'Why is it you're so determined to suspect my motives?' Alex asked.

'You're a man,' Beth told him acidly, 'and my experience of men is that...' She looked away from him. Something about the tight white line around Alex's mouth was hurting her. Without knowing how it had happened she had strayed onto some very treacherous and uncertain ground indeed.

'So, I'm to be condemned without a hearing, is that it? Who was he, Beth?' he asked her grimly. 'A friend? A lover?'

'Actually he was neither,' she told him. Frantically she got up, but she had only taken a few steps before he caught up with her and swung her round to face him.

Beneath her fingertips Beth could feel the fabric of his shirt, soft and warm, but the body that lay beneath it felt deliciously firm...hard, masculine, an unfamiliar and even forbidden territory that her fingers were suddenly dangerously eager

Dear Reader

Revenge is a very strong emotion. The need to seek it and the act of avenging a wrongdoing is very empowering. The four women in this, my latest mini-series, all have to learn to handle this most powerful of emotions, in her own special way.

I am aware of the dangers of people becoming blinded to everything but one single, obsessive goal. As I wrote these books, I discovered that my heroines, Kelly, Anna, Beth and Dee, all share my instincts. Like me, they desperately want to see justice done but, also like me, they come to recognise that there is an even stronger drive—love can conquer all.

These four women share a bond of friendship and it is very much in my mind when I write that you, the reader, and I, the writer, also share a very special and personal bond. I invite you to share in the lives, hopes and loves of Kelly, Anna, Beth and Dee. Through love they will discover true happiness.

Love, laughter and friendship—life holds no greater joys and I wish you all of them and more.

Penny Jordan

Sweet Revenge
Seduction

They wanted to get even. Instead they got married!

Look for Dee's story
Coming next from Penny Jordan

A TREACHEROUS SEDUCTION

BY
PENNY JORDAN

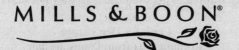

MILLS & BOON®

In memory of Dagmar Digrinová
whose enthusiasm and love
for her country inspired
this book.

*First published in Great Britain 1999
Harlequin Mills & Boon Limited,
Eton House, 18-24 Paradise Road, Richmond, Surrey TW9 1SR*

© Penny Jordan 1999

ISBN 0 263 81741 5

*Set in Times Roman 10½ on 12 pt.
01-9908-48502 C1*

*Printed and bound in Spain
by Litografia Rosés, S.A., Barcelona*

CHAPTER ONE

BETH gave an involuntary gasp of horrified disbelief as she stared white-faced at the contents of the crate she had just opened.

'Oh, no! *No!*' she protested in despair as she picked up the wine glass she had just removed from its packaging, one of a suite of matching stemware she had ordered on her buying trip to Prague.

Beth closed her eyes; her face had gone deathly pale and she felt rather sick.

She had invested so much in this Czech order, and not just in terms of money.

Her fingers trembling, she opened another box, biting her bottom lip hard as the decorative water jug she had in her hand confirmed all her growing anxiety.

Three hours later, with the storeroom at the back of the small shop she ran in partnership with her best friend Kelly Frobisher strewn with packages and stemware, all Beth's worst fears were realised.

These…these abominations against good taste and style were most certainly not the deliciously pretty reproduction antique items *she* had ordered with such excitement and pleasure all those months ago in the Czech Republic. No way. *This* order, the order she had received but most certainly never placed, might equate in terms of numbers and suites to what she had bought, but in every other way it was horrendous, horrible, a parody of the beautiful, elegant,

5

covetable top-quality stemware she had seen and paid for.

No, there was no way she would ever have ordered anything like this, and no way could she ever sell it either. Her customers were very discriminating, and Beth's stomach churned as she recalled how enthusiastically and confidently she had titillated their interest by describing her order to them and promising them that it would turn their Christmas dinner tables into wonderful facsimiles of a bygone age, an age of Venetian baroque, Byzantine beauty.

Sickly she stared at the glass she was holding, a glass she remembered as being a richly gorgeous Christmassy cranberry-red with a depth of colour one could almost eat.

Was it really for this that she had put the small shop, her reputation and her personal finances into jeopardy? Was it for *this* that she had telephoned her bank manager from Prague to persuade him to extend her credit facilities? No, of course it wasn't. The glassware she had been shown had been nothing like this. Nothing at all!

Feverishly she examined another piece, and then another, hoping against hope that what she had already seen had simply been a slight mistake. But there was no mistake. Everything she unpacked possessed the same hallmarks of poor workmanship, inferior glass and crude colouring. The blue she remembered as being the same deep, wonderful colour as a Renaissance painter's Madonna's robes, as having the same depth when held up to the light as the most beautiful of antique stained-glass windows, the green she recalled as possessing the depth and fire of a high-quality emerald, and the gold which had

had gilding as subtle as anything to come out of an expert gilder's workshop were, in reality, like comparing the colours in a child's paintbox to those used by a true artist.

There had to have been a mistake. Beth stood up. She would have to ring the suppliers and advise them of their error.

Her brain went into frantic overdrive as she tried to grapple with the enormity of the problem now confronting her. After being delayed well beyond its original delivery date, the order had just barely arrived in time for their Christmas market.

In fact, she had planned this very afternoon to clear the shelves of their current stock and restock them with the Czech stemware.

What on earth was she going to do?

Normally this would have been a problem she would immediately have shared with her partner, Kelly, but these were not normal circumstances. For one thing, she had been in Prague on her own when she had taken the initiative to order the stemware. For a second, Kelly was quite rightly far more preoccupied with her new husband and the life they were establishing together than she was with the shop at the moment, and they had mutually agreed that for the time being Kelly would take a back seat in the business they had started up together in the small town of Rye-on-Averton, where the girls had originally been encouraged to come by Beth's godmother, Anna Trewayne.

And for a third...

Beth closed her eyes. She knew that if she were to tell her godmother, Anna, or Kelly, her best friend, or even Dee Lawson, her landlady, of the financial and professional mess she was now in all three of them would immediately rush to her aid, full of understanding and sympathy for her plight. But Beth was sharply conscious of the fact that, out of the four of them, she was the only one who always seemed to get things wrong, who always seemed to make bad judgements, who always seemed to end up being duped…cheated…hurt. Who always seemed to be a loser…a victim…

Beth shuddered with a mixture of anger and anguish. What was the *matter* with her? *Why* was she constantly involving herself with people who ultimately let her down? She might, as other people were constantly reminding her, be placid, and perhaps a little too on the accommodating side, but that didn't mean that she didn't have any pride, that she didn't need to be treated with respect.

None of the other three would have got themselves in this situation, she was sure. Dee, for instance, would most certainly not have done. No, she couldn't imagine anyone ever managing to dupe or cheat Dee, with her confident, businesslike manner, nor Kelly, with her vibrant, positive personality, nor even Anna, with her quiet gentleness.

No, *she* was the vulnerable one, the fool, the idiot, who had 'cheat me' written all over her.

It had to be her own fault. Look at the way she had fallen for Julian Cox's lies; look how gullible she had been, believing that he loved her when all the time what he had really been interested in had been the money he had believed she would inherit.

She had been stricken with shame when Julian had left her, claiming that he had never told her that he wanted to marry her, accusing her of running after him, pursuing him, of imagining that he had ever felt something for her.

Beth's face started to burn. Not because she still loved him—she most certainly didn't, and she doubted deep in her heart that she ever had; she had simply allowed him to persuade her that she had, because she had been flattered by the assiduous attentions he had paid her, and by his constant declarations of love, his insistence that they were soul mates. Well, she had certainly learned her lesson there. Never, ever again would she trust a man who treated her like that, who claimed to have fallen crazily and instantly in love with her as Julian had done, and she had stuck to that private vow even when...

Beth could feel her heart starting to thud heavily as she fought to suppress certain dangerous memories.

At least she hadn't made the *same* mistake twice. No, she agreed mentally with herself, she'd just gone on to make fresh ones.

A failed romance and the public humiliation of other people knowing about it, painful though it had been, had at least only damaged her own life. What had happened now had the potential to humiliate not just her but Kelly as well.

They had built up a very good reputation in the town since opening their crystal and china shop. Because they were a small outlet they concentrated on matching their customers' needs and, where they could, innovatively anticipating them.

Kelly had already told her enthusiastically that they had several very good customers, with celebrations of one sort or another coming up, to whom she had mentioned the fact that the purchase of some very special and individual stemware might be an excellent idea.

One customer in particular had been talking excitedly to Beth only the previous week about purchasing three dozen of the crimson Czech champagne flutes.

'It's our silver wedding this year—two days before Christmas—the whole family will be coming to us and it would be wonderful to have the glasses for then. I'm having a large family dinner party and we could use them for the champagne cocktails I'm planning to do, and for the toasts...'

'Oh, yes, they would be perfect,' Beth had enthused, already in her mind's eye seeing them on her customer's antique dining table, the delicacy of the fragile glass and the richness of the colour emphasised by the candlelight.

There was no way Candida Lewis-Benton would want to order what she, Beth, had just unpacked. No way at all.

Valiantly Beth fought the temptation to burst into tears. She was a woman, not a girl, and, as she had thought she had proved when she was in Prague, she could be determined and self-reliant and, yes, proud too. She could earn her *own* self-respect, and never mind what certain other people thought of her—certain other not-to-be-thought-of, or thought *about*, arrogant, overbearing men who thought they knew her better than she knew herself. Who wanted to take over her life and her, who thought they could lie to her and get her to acquiesce to whatever they wanted for her by claiming that they loved her. And she had known, of course, just what it was *he* had wanted.

Well, she had at least shown him just how easily she had seen through his duplicitous behaviour.

'Beth, I know it's probably too soon to tell you this, but I…I've fallen in love with you,' he had told her that afternoon in the pouring rain on the Charles Bridge.

'No, that's not possible,' she had replied hardily.

'If that wasn't love, then just exactly what was it?' he had demanded on another occasion, and he had touched his fingertips to her lips, still swollen and soft from the passion they had just exchanged.

She had answered boldly, 'It was just lust—just sex, that's all…' And she had gone on to prove it to him.

'Don't be tempted into falling for the promises these street traders make to you,' he had warned her more than once. 'They're simply pawns being used by organised crime to dupe tourists.'

She knew quite well what he'd been after. What *he'd* been after was exactly what Julian had been after—her money. Only Alex Andrews had wanted her body thrown in as well.

At least sexually Julian had done the decent thing, so to speak.

'I don't want us to be lovers…not yet…not until you're wearing my ring,' Julian had whispered passionately to her the night he had declared his love— a love he had not felt for her at all, as it later transpired.

It seemed almost laughable now that she had ever agonised so much over his perfidy. Perhaps the acute sense of self-loathing she had experienced over his betrayal and accusations had had more to do with the humiliation he had made her suffer rather than a genuinely broken heart.

Certainly, whenever she thought about him now, which was rarely, it was without any emotion whatsoever other than a distant sense of amazement that she could ever have considered him attractive. She had gone to Prague determined to prove to herself that she was not the emotional fool Julian had painted her as being, vowing that never again would she let herself be conned into believing that when a man told her he loved her he meant it.

She had come back from Prague feeling extremely proud of herself, and equally proud of the new, hard-headed, hard-hearted Beth she had turned herself into. If men wanted to lie to her and betray her, then she would learn to play them at their own game. She was an adult woman, with all that that encompassed. Mistrusting men as emotional partners didn't mean that she had to deny herself the pleasure of finding them sexually desirable. The days were gone when a woman had to deny the sexual side of her nature. The days had gone, too, when a woman had to convince herself that she loved a man and that, even more important, he loved and respected her before she could give herself to him physically.

She had been living in the Dark Ages, Beth had told herself—living her life by an outdated set of rules and an even more outdated set of moral beliefs. An outdated and far too idealistic set of moral beliefs. Well, all that was over now. Now she had finally joined the real world, the world of harsh realities. Now she was a fully paid-up member of modern society, and if men, or rather a certain man, did not like the things she did or the things she said, then tough. The right to enjoy sex for sex's sake was no longer a purely male province, and if Alex Andrews didn't like that fact then it was just too bad.

Had he really thought she was going to fall for those lies he had told her? All those ridiculous claims he had made about falling in love with her the moment he first saw her?

Prague had been surprisingly full of people like him. British- and American-born in the main, students, most of them, or so they'd claimed, taking a year out to 'do' areas previously off limits to them. Some had family connections in the Czech Republic, some not, but all of them had possessed a common ingredient; all of them, to some extent, had been living off their wits, using their skills as linguists, charming a living out of gullible tourists. In Beth's newly cynical opinion they'd been only one step removed from the high-pressure-sales types hawking time-share apartments, who had made certain holiday areas of the continent notorious until their governments had taken steps to control their activities.

True, Alex Andrews had alluded to the very different lifestyle he claimed to lead in Britain. According to his own description of himself he was a university lecturer in Modern History at a prestigious university college who was taking a sabbatical to spend some time with the Czech side of his family, but Beth hadn't believed him. Why should she have? Julian Cox had claimed to have a highly profitable and respectable financial empire—he had turned out to be little more than a fraudster who had somehow managed to keep himself one step in front of actually breaking the law. It had been plain to Beth from the first moment she had met him that Alex Andrews was very much the same type.

Too good-looking, too self-confident...too sure that she'd been going to fall into his arms just because he claimed he was desperate to have her there. She wasn't *that* much of a fool. She might have fallen for that kind of line once, but she certainly hadn't been about to fall for it a second time.

Oh, yes, she had escaped making a fool of herself over Alex Andrews, but she hadn't been able to prevent herself from...

Numbly Beth studied the stemware she had unpacked. There was a sick, shaky feeling in her stomach, a sensation of mingled panic and dread. It had to be a mistake... It *had* to be.

She simply couldn't face telling Dee, Anna and Kelly that she had made a spectacularly bad error of judgement—again.

And she certainly couldn't face telling her bank manager. She had really gone out on a limb with the loan she had persuaded him to give her—and she it.

Anxiously she got to her feet. The first thing she needed to do was to ring the factory.

She was just about to dial the number on her invoice when the telephone rang. Picking up the receiver, she heard her partner Kelly's voice.

'Beth, you're going to hate me for this...' Kelly paused. 'Brough is having to go to Singapore on business and he wants me to go with him. It could mean us being away for over a month—he says that since we would be almost halfway there anyway we might as well also fly on to Australia and spend a couple of weeks with my cousin and her family.

'I know what you must be thinking. We're coming

up for our busiest time and I've only been working a couple of days a week lately anyway. If you'd rather I didn't go I'll understand... After all, the business...'

Beth thought quickly. It was true that she *would* find it hard to manage for what sounded as though it was going to be close on five or six weeks without her partner, but if Kelly was away then at least it meant that Beth wouldn't have to tell her about the stemware. Cravenly Beth admitted to herself that, given the opportunity to do so, she would much rather sort out everything discreetly and privately without involving anyone else—even if that meant getting someone in part-time to help with the shop whilst Kelly was away.

'Beth? Are you still there?' she heard Kelly asking her anxiously.

'Yes. Yes, I'm here,' Beth confirmed.

Taking a deep breath, she told her friend and partner as cheerfully as she could, 'Of course you must go, Kelly. It would be silly to miss out on that kind of opportunity.'

'Mmm...and I would miss Brough dreadfully. But I do feel guilty about leaving you, Beth, especially at this time of the year. I know how busy you're going to be, what with the new stemware... Oh...did it arrive? Is it as wonderful as you remembered? Perhaps I could come down...?'

'No. No...there's no need for that,' Beth assured her quickly.

'Well, if you really don't mind,' Kelly said gratefully. 'Brough did say that we could drive over to Farrow today. I've been given the address of someone who works there who makes the most wonderful traditional hand-crafted furniture. He's got one of those purpose-built workshops in the Old Hall Stables there. It's been turned into a small craft village. But if you need me at the shop…'

'No. I'm fine,' Beth assured her.

'When are you putting the new stemware stuff out?' Kelly asked enthusiastically. 'I'm dying to see it…'

Beth tensed.

'Er…I haven't decided yet…'

'Oh. I thought you said you were going to do it as soon as it arrived,' Kelly protested, plainly confused.

'Yes. I was. But…but I want to get a few more ideas yet; we've still got nearly a fortnight before the town's Christmas lights and decorations are in place, and I thought it would be a good idea to time the window to fit in with that…'

'Oh, yes, that's a wonderful idea,' Kelly enthused. 'We could even have a small wine and nibbles do for our customers…perhaps have the food and the drinks the same colour as the glass…'

'Er…yes. Yes…that would be wonderful,' Beth agreed, hoping that her voice didn't sound as lacking in enthusiasm to her friend as it did to herself.

'Oh, but I've just realised; we'll be leaving at the end of the week so I shall miss it,' Kelly complained. 'Still, we'll definitely be back for Christmas; that's something I have insisted on to Brough, and fortunately he agrees with me that our first Christmas should be spent here at home…together… Which reminds me. Please save me a set of those wonderful glasses, Beth.'

'Er, yes, I shall,' Beth confirmed.

With luck, she would be able to get the mistake in her order reversed and the correct stemware sent out to her whilst Kelly was away. Whilst Kelly was away, yes, but would she get it in time for the all-important Christmas market? When selecting the pieces for her order she had deliberately focused on the colours she deemed to be the most saleable for the Christmas season; deep red, rich blue, fir-tree green, all in the lavishly baroque style and decorated with gold leaf. Beautiful though the pieces were, she doubted that they would have the same sales appeal in the spring and summer months.

One hour and five unanswered telephone calls after she had finished speaking with Kelly, Beth sat back on her heels and stared helplessly around her chaotic storeroom.

The horror and the anger she had initially felt at having received the wrong order were giving way even more to frantic unease and suspicion.

The factory she had visited had been a large one, and the sales director she had spoken with suave and business-suited. The cabinets which had lined the walls of his plush office had been filled with the almost mouth-wateringly beautiful stemware from which he had invited Beth to take her choice for her order.

His secretary's office, which she had glimpsed through an open door as he had escorted her from the reception foyer and into his own office, had been crammed with the most up-to-the-minute modern technology, and it was just not feasible that such an organisation would not, during office hours, have its telephone system fully manned and its faxes working.

But every time Beth had punched the numbers into her own telephone she had been met with a blank silence, an emptiness humming along the wire. Even if the factory had been closed for the Czech Republic version of a Bank Holiday, the telephone would still have rung.

The most horrible suspicion, the most awful possibility, was beginning to edge its way into Beth's thoughts.

'Don't be taken in by what you've been shown,' Alex Andrews had warned her. 'Some gypsies are thought to be used as pawns in organised crime. Their aim is to sell non-existent goods to gullible foreign tourists in order to bring into the organisation foreign currency.'

'I don't believe you. You're just trying to frighten me,' Beth had told him furiously. 'To frighten me and to make sure that I give my order to your cousins,' she had added sharply. '*That's* what all this is really about, isn't it? Telling me you've fallen in love with me...claiming to care about me... I *would* be gullible if I had fallen for your lies, Alex...'

Beth didn't want to remember Alex's reaction to her accusations. She didn't want to remember anything about Alex Andrews at all. She wasn't going to allow herself to remember *anything* about him.

No? Then how come she had dreamed about him virtually every night since her return from the Czech Republic? a small inner voice taunted her.

She had dreamed about him simply out of the relief of knowing she had stood by her own promises to herself and not fallen for his lies, his claims to love her, Beth told her unwanted internal critic crossly.

She looked at her watch. It was almost four o'clock. No point in trying the Czech suppliers again today. Instead she would repack her incorrect order.

Dee, their landlady for the shop and the comfortable accommodation that went with it, who had now become a good friend, had invited her over for supper this evening.

Dispiritedly she started to repack the stemware, shuddering a little as she did so. The crystal was more suitable for jam jars than stemware, Beth decided with a grimace of distaste.

'Haven't I heard,' Dee had queried gently a few weeks ago, 'that some of the processes through which their china and glassware are made are a little crude when compared to ours...?'

'At the lower end of the market perhaps they are,' Beth had defended. 'But this factory I found originally actually made things for the Royal House of Russia. The sales director showed me the most exquisite pieces of a dinner service they'd had made for one of the Romanian Princes. It reminded me very much of a Sèvres service, and the translucency of the china was quite breathtaking. The Czech people are very proud of their tradition of making high-quality crystal,' Beth had added.

She had Alex Andrews to thank for *that* little piece of information. It had been something he had thrown furiously at her when she had accused him of trying to persuade her to buy his cousins' goods, and the cause of yet another quarrel between them.

Beth had never met anyone who infuriated her as much as he had done. He had brought out in her a streak of anger and passion she had never previously known she possessed.

Anger and passion. Two very dangerous emotions.

Quickly Beth got back to repacking the open crates. Remember, she told herself sternly, you aren't going to think about him. *Or* about what…what happened…

To her chagrin, Beth could feel her face starting to heat and then burn.

'God, but you're wonderful. So sweet and gentle on the outside and so hot and wild in private, so very hot and wild…'

Furious with herself, Beth jumped up.

'You weren't going to think about him,' she told herself fiercely. 'You *aren't* going to think about him.'

CHAPTER TWO

'MORE coffee, Beth…?'

'Mmm…'

'You seem rather preoccupied. Is anything wrong?' Dee asked Beth in concern as she put down the coffee pot she had been holding.

They had finished eating and were now sitting in Dee's sitting room, where several furnishing and decorating catalogues were spread open around them. Dee was planning to redecorate the room, and had been asking Beth for her opinion of the choices she had made.

'No. No…I like the cream brocade very much,' Beth told Dee quickly. 'And if you opt for the cream carpet as well, that will allow you to bring in some richer, stronger colours in the form of cushions and throws…'

'Yes, that was what I was thinking. I've seen a wonderful fabric that I've really fallen for, and I've managed to track down the manufacturer, but it's a very small company. They've told me that they can only accept my order if I pay for it up front, and of course I'm reluctant to do that, just in case they can't or don't deliver.

'I've asked my bank to run a financial check on them and let me have the results. It will be a pity if the report isn't favourable. The fabric is wonderful, and I've really set my heart on it. But of course one has to be cautious in these matters, as no doubt you know.

'You must have really been keeping your fingers crossed in Prague whilst you waited for your bank to verify that the Czech company was financially sound enough for you to do business with.'

'Er…yes. Yes, I was…'

Beth took a quick gulp of her coffee.

What would Dee say if Beth were to admit to her that she had done no such thing, that she had quite simply been so excited at the thought of selling the wonderful stemware she had seen that every principle of financial caution she had ever learnt had flown right out of her head?

'Kelly rang me today. She was telling me that she and Brough are hoping to make an extended trip to Singapore and Australia…'

'Mmm…they are,' Beth agreed.

She *ought* to have asked her bank to make proper enquiries over the Czech factory. She knew that, of course. Not just to ensure that they were financially sound, but also to find out how good they were at meeting their order dates. She could even remember her bank manager advising that she do so when she had telephoned him to ask him for extra credit facilities. And no doubt if he hadn't been on the point of departing for his annual leave on the very afternoon she had rung *he* would have made sure that she had done so.

But he had and she hadn't and the small, nagging little seed of doubt planted earlier by her inability to make telephone or fax contact with the factory was now throwing out shoots and roots of increasingly strong suspicion and dread with frightening speed.

'How will you manage whilst Kelly's away? You'll have to get someone in part-time to help you...'

'Yes. Yes, I shall,' Beth agreed distractedly, wondering half hysterically what on earth Dee would say if she admitted to her that, if her worst fears were confirmed and her incorrect order had not been a mistake but a deliberate and cynical ploy to take advantage of her there was no way she would *need* any extra sales staff because, quite simply, there would be virtually nothing in the shop to sell.

Another fear sprang into Beth's thoughts. If she had nothing to sell then how was she going to pay her rent on the shop and the living accommodation above it?

She had absolutely nothing to fall back on, not now that she had over-extended herself so dangerously to purchase the Czech glass.

Her parents would always help her out, she knew that, and so, too, she suspected, would Anna, her godmother. But how could she go to any of them and admit how foolish she had been?

No, she had got herself into this mess, and somehow she would get herself out of it.

And her first step in doing that was to locate her supplier and insist that the factory take back her incorrect order and supply her with the goods she had actually ordered.

'Beth, are you *sure* you're all right...?'

Guiltily she realised that Dee had been speaking to her and that she hadn't registered a single word that the older woman had been saying.

'Er...yes...I'm fine...'

'Well, if it would be any help I could always come and relieve you at the shop for the odd half-day.'

'*You!*' Beth stared at Dee in astonishment, surprised to see that Dee was actually flushing.

'You needn't sound quite so surprised,' Dee told Beth slightly defensively. 'I *did* actually work in a shop while I was at university.'

Had she hurt Dee's feelings? Beth tried not to show her surprise. Dee always seemed so armoured and self-contained, but there was quite definitely a decidedly hurt look in her eyes.

'If I sounded surprised it was just because I know how busy you already are,' Beth assured her truthfully.

Dee's late father had had an extensive business empire which Dee had taken over following his death, managing not only the large amounts of money her father had built up through shrewd investment but also administering the various charity accounts he had set up to help those in need in the town.

Dee's father had been the old-fashioned kind of philanthropist, very much in the Victorian vein, wanting to benefit his neighbours and fellow townspeople.

He had been a traditionalist in many other ways as well, from what Beth had heard about him—a regular churchgoer throughout his life and a loving father who had brought Dee up on his own after his wife's premature death.

Dee was passionately devoted to preserving her father's memory, and whenever anyone praised her for the good work she did via the charities she helped to fund she was always quick to point out that she was simply acting as her father's representative.

When Beth and Kelly had first moved to the town they had wondered curiously why Dee had never married. She had to be about thirty, and surprisingly for such a businesslike and shrewd woman she had a very strong maternal streak. She was also very attractive.

'Perhaps she just hasn't found the right man,' Beth had suggested to Kelly. That had been in the days when she herself had believed that she had very much found the right man, in the shape of Julian Cox, and had therefore been disposed to feel extremely sorry for anyone who was not so similarly blessed.

'Mmm…or maybe no man can compare in her eyes to her father,' Kelly had guessed, more shrewdly.

Whatever the truth, one thing was certain: Dee was simply not the kind of person whose private life one could pry into uninvited. And yet tonight she seemed unfamiliarly vulnerable; she even looked softer, and somehow younger as well, Beth noticed. Perhaps because she had left her hair down out of its normal stylish coil.

Certainly it would be impossible to overlook her, even in a crowd. She had the kind of looks, the kind of manner that immediately commanded other people's attention—unlike *her*, Beth decided with wry self-disdain.

Her soft mousy-blonde hair would never attract a second look, not even when the sun had left it, as it had done last summer, with these lighter delicate streaks in it.

As a teenager she had passionately longed to grow taller. At five feet four she was undeniably short... 'Petite', Julian had once infamously called her. Petite and as prettily delicate as a fragile porcelain doll. And she had thought he was *complimenting* her. Yuck. She was short. But she was very slender, and she did have a softness about her, an air which had once unforgettably and almost unforgivably led Kelly to say that she could almost have modelled for the book *Little Women*'s Beth.

On impulse, before going to Prague, she had had her long hair shaped and cut. The chopped, blunt-edged bob suited her, even if sometimes she did find it irritating, and had to tuck the stray ends behind her ears to stop them from falling over her face when she was working.

'You are beautiful,' Alex Andrews had told her extravagantly when he had held her in his arms. 'The most beautiful woman in the whole world.'

She had known that he was lying, of course, and why, and she hadn't been deceived—no, not for one minute—despite the sharp, twisting knife-like pain she had felt as she had listened to him in the full knowledge of his duplicity.

Why would he possibly think she was beautiful? After all, he was a man who any woman could see was quite extraordinarily handsome in a way that was far more classical Greek god than modern-day film star. Tall, with a body that possessed a steely whip-cord-fit muscular strength, he'd seemed to radiate a fierce and very high-charged air of sensual magnetism that had almost been like some kind of personal force field. Impossible to ignore it—or him. Beth had felt at times as though he was draining the will-power out of her, as though he was somehow subtly overpowering her with the intensity of his sexual aura.

He also had the most remarkably hypnotic silver-grey eyes. She could see them now, feel their heat burning her. She could…

'Beth…?'

'I'm sorry Dee,' she apologised guiltily.

'It's all right,' Dee assured her, with her unexpectedly wide and warm smile. 'Kelly told me that you'd collected your stemware from the airport and that you were unpacking it. I must say that I'm looking forward to seeing it. I've got some spare time tomorrow. Perhaps if I called round…?'

Beth could feel herself starting to panic.

'Er…I don't want anyone to see it until the town's Christmas lights go on officially,' she told Dee quickly. 'I haven't got it on the shelves yet, and—'

'You want to surprise everyone by making a wonderful display with it,' Dee guessed, her smile broadening.

'Well, whatever you decide to do with it, to display it, I know it's going to look wonderful. You really do have a very creative and artistic eye,' she complimented Beth truthfully, adding ruefully, 'And I most certainly do not. Which is why I needed your advice on the refurbishment of my sitting room.'

'Your eye is actually very good,' Beth assured her. 'It's just when it comes to those extra details that you need a bit of help. That crimson damask trimmed with the dull gold fringing would make a wonderful throw…'

'It'll be very rich,' Dee commented doubtfully.

'Yes, it will,' Beth agreed. 'Perfect for winter, and

then for spring and summer you could switch to something softer. Your sitting room French windows open out onto the garden, and a throw which picks up the colours in that bed you've got within view of the window would be a perfect way to bring the garden and the sitting room into harmony with one another.'

Beth glanced at her watch and stood up. It was time for her to leave.

'Don't forget,' Dee urged her, 'if you *do* need some help in the shop, let me know. I realise that Anna sometimes stands in, when either you or Kelly aren't available, but...'

She stopped as Beth was already shaking her head.

'There's no way that Ward will allow Anna to spend several hours on her feet right now. Anna says that you'd think no woman had ever had a baby before. Apparently it doesn't matter how often she tells him that being pregnant is a perfectly natural state, that she's happy and there's absolutely nothing for him to worry about; he still treats her as though she's too fragile to draw breath.'

Dee laughed ruefully.

'He's certainly very protective of her. He was most disapproving the other day when he found out she and I'd been to the garden centre and that I'd let her carry a box of plants. But then I suspect he still hasn't completely forgiven me for sending him away when he came to look for Anna before they were married.'

'You were only trying to protect her,' Beth protested. She liked Ward, and was pleased that her godmother had found happiness with him after being widowed for so long, but she could well understand how two such strong characters as Dee and Ward would clash occasionally.

Only a very, very fine line separated a strong, determined man from being a bossy, domineering one, as she had good cause to know. Ward, fortunately, knew which side of the line to be on; Alex Andrews did not.

Alex Andrews.

He would certainly have enjoyed her present predicament, *and* he would have enjoyed even more saying 'I told you so' to her.

Alex Andrews!

Beth parked her small car outside the shop and let herself into the separate rear door which led upstairs to the living accommodation she had originally shared with Kelly.

Alex Andrews!

She was *still* thinking about him as she made herself a cup of tea and headed for her bedroom.

Alex Andrews—or, more correctly, Alex Charles Andrews.

'I was named for this bridge,' he had told her quietly the day they had stood together on Prague's fabled Charles Bridge. 'A reminder, my grandfather always used to say, of the fact that I was half Czech.'

'Is that why you're here?' Beth had asked him, curious despite her determination to remain aloof from him—aloof *from* him and suspicious *of* him.

'Yes,' he acknowledged simply. 'My parents came here in the early days after the Velvet Revolution in 1993.' His eyes had grown sombre. 'Unfortunately my grandfather died too soon to see the city he had always loved freed.

'He left Prague in 1946 with my grandmother and

my mother, who was a child of two at the time. She can barely remember anything at all about living here, but my grandfather...' He stopped and shook his head, and Beth felt her own throat close up as she saw the glitter of tears in his eyes.

'He longed to come back here so much. It was his home, after all, and no matter how well he had settled in England, how *glad* he was to be able to bring up his daughter, my mother, in freedom, Prague always remained the home of his heart.

'I remember once when I was at Cambridge he came to see me and I took him punting on the Cam. "It's beautiful," he told me. "But it isn't anywhere near as beautiful as the river which flows through Prague. Not until you have stood on the Charles Bridge and seen it for yourself will you understand what I mean..."'

'And did you?' Beth asked him softly. 'Did you understand what he meant?'

'Yes,' Alex told her quietly. 'Until I came here I had thought of myself as wholly British. I knew of my Czech heritage of course, but only in the form of the stories my grandfather had told me.

'They had no substance, no reality for me other than *as* stories. The tales he told me of the castle his family had once owned and the land that went with it, the beautiful treasures and the fine furniture...' Alex gave a small shrug. 'I felt no sense of personal loss. How could I? And neither did I feel any personal sense of missing a part of myself. But once I came here—then...then...yes... I knew that there *was* a piece of me missing. Then I knew that subconsciously I had been searching for that missing piece of myself.'

'Will you stay here?' Beth asked him, drawn into the emotional intensity of what he was telling her in spite of herself.

'No,' Alex told her. 'I can't—not now.'

It was then that the heavens well and truly opened, causing him to grab her by the arm and run with her to the shelter of a small, dangerously private alcove tucked into a span of the bridge. And then that he had declared his love for her.

Immediately Beth panicked—it was too much, too soon, too impossible to believe. He must have some ulterior motive for saying such a thing to her. How could he be in love with *her?* Why should he be?

'*No!* No, that's not possible. I don't want to hear this, Alex,' she told him shortly, pulling away from him and out of the shelter of the alcove, leaving him to follow her.

Beth had first come across Alex at her hotel. The staff there, when she had asked for the services of an interpreter, had prevaricated and then informed Beth that, due to the fact that the city was currently hosting several large business conventions, all the reputable agencies were fully booked for days ahead. Beth's heart had sunk. There was no way she could do what she had come to the Czech Republic to do without the services of an interpreter, and she had said as much to the young man behind the hotel's reception desk.

'I am so very sorry,' the man apologised, spreading his hands helplessly. 'But there are no interpreters.'

No interpreters. Beth was perilously close to tears; her emotions, still raw in the aftermath of discovering how badly Julian Cox had deceived her, were inclined to fluctuate from the easy weepiness of someone still in shock to a numb blankness which, if anything, was even more frightening. Today was a weepy day, and as Beth fought to blink away her unwanted emotions through the watery haze of her tears she saw the man who had been standing several feet away from her at the counter turn towards her.

'I couldn't help overhearing what you were just saying,' he told Beth as she turned to walk away from the desk. 'And, although I know it's rather unorthodox, I was wondering if *I* could possibly be of any help to you...'

His English was so fluent that Beth knew immediately that it had to be his first language.

'You're English, aren't you?' she challenged him dubiously.

'By birth,' he agreed immediately, giving her a smile which could have disarmed a nuclear warhead.

Beth, though, as she firmly reminded herself, was made of sterner stuff. There was no way *she* was going to let any man, never mind one who possessed enough charisma to make him worthy of having a 'danger' sign posted across his forehead, wheedle his way into her life.

'I speak English myself,' Beth told him pleasantly and, of course, unnecessarily.

'Indeed, and with just a hint of a very pretty Cornish accent, if I may say so,' he astounded Beth by commenting with a grin. 'However,' he added, before she could fire back, 'it seems that you do *not* speak Czech, whereas I do...'

'Really?' Beth gave him a coolly dismissive smile and began to walk away from him. She had been warned about the dangers of employing one of the self-proclaimed guides and interpreters who offered their services on Prague's streets, approaching tourists and offering to help them.

'Mmm…I learned it from my grandfather. He came originally from Prague.'

Beth tensed as he fell into step beside her.

'Ah, I see what it is. You don't trust me. Very wise,' he approved, with astounding aplomb. 'A beautiful young woman like you, on her own in a strange city, should always be suspicious of men who approach her.'

Beth glowered at him. Just how gullible did he think she was?

'I am not…' Beautiful, she had been about to say, but, recognising her danger, she quickly changed it. 'I am not interested.'

'No? But you told the receptionist that you were *desperately* in need of an interpreter,' he reminded her softly. 'The hotel manager will, I am sure, vouch for me…'

Beth paused.

He was right about one thing: she *was* desperately in need of an interpreter. She had come to Prague partially to recover from the damage inflicted on her emotions by Julian Cox and, more importantly in her eyes at least, in order to buy some good-quality Czech stemware for her shop.

Via Dee she had obtained from their local Board of Trade some addresses and contacts, but she had been told that the best way to find what she was looking for was to make her own enquiries once she was in Prague, and there was no way she was going to be able to do that without some help. It wasn't just an interpreter she needed, she acknowledged; she needed a guide as well. Someone who could drive her to the various factories she needed to visit as well as translating for her once she was there.

'Why should *you* offer to help me?' she asked suspiciously.

'Perhaps I simply don't have any choice,' he responded with an enigmatic smile.

The smile Beth dismissed. As for his comment— perhaps he hoped to make her feel sorry for him by insinuating that he was short of money.

Whilst she was still wondering just what she ought to do a very elegant dark-haired woman in her early fifties came hurrying down the corridor towards them.

'Ah, Alex, there you are!' she exclaimed, addressing Beth's companion. 'If you're ready to leave, the car's here…'

She gave Beth a coolly assessing look which made Beth feel acutely conscious of her own casual clothes and the older woman's immaculate elegance. She had the chicness of a Parisian, from the tips of her immaculately manicured fingernails to the top of her shiningly groomed chignon. Pearls, large enough to have been fake but which Beth felt pretty sure were anything but, were clipped to her ears, and the gold necklace she was wearing looked equally expensive.

Whoever she was, the woman was obviously very wealthy. If this man was acting as an interpreter for her he *must* be trustworthy, Beth acknowledged, because one look at the older woman's face made it abundantly clear that she was not the sort of person to be duped by anyone—no matter how handsome their face or how sexy their body.

'You don't have to make up your mind right now,' the man was telling Beth calmly. 'Here is my name and a number where you can reach me.' Reaching into his jacket, he removed a pen and a piece of paper on which he quickly wrote something before handing it to Beth. 'I shall be here in the hotel tomorrow morning. You can let me know your decision then.'

She wasn't going to accept his offer, of course, Beth assured herself once he and his companion had gone. Even if he had been an accredited interpreter provided by a reputable agency she would still have had her doubts.

Because he's too sexy...too...too disturbingly male, and you're too vulnerable, an inner voice taunted her. I thought you were supposed to be immune to men like him now. You said that Julian Cox had cured you of ever falling in love again.

No. That will never happen, she answered her sharp-tongued inner critic swiftly. There's no way I could ever be in danger of falling for a man like him, a man who's far too good-looking for his own good. Heavens, he must have women swarming all over him. Why on earth should he be interested in someone like me?

Perhaps for the same reason that Julian Cox was interested in you, her inner critic taunted. To him you probably seem to be an easy meal ticket. A woman on her own, vulnerable. Remember what you were told before you left home.

Beth was determined not to accept Alex's offer, but in the morning, when she presented herself at the hotel's reception desk again, insisting that she desperately needed an accredited interpreter, the man behind the counter shook his head regretfully, repeating what Beth had been told the previous day.

'I am sorry, but we simply cannot. There are conventions,' he told Beth.

It crossed Beth's mind that she might have to abandon her plans to make this a business trip and simply do some sightseeing instead. But that would mean going home, having to admit to another failure… She had come to Prague to look for crystal, and she was not going to go home until she had found some.

Even if that meant accepting the services of a man like Alex Andrews?

Even if it meant accepting that—*yes!* Beth told herself sternly.

She had eaten her breakfast alone in her room; the hotel was busy, and, despite all the stern admonishments she had made to herself, she still didn't feel confident enough to eat in the dining room—alone. Now she ordered herself a coffee and removed the guidebook she had bought on her arrival in Prague from her handbag. For all she knew Alex Andrews might not even turn up. Well, if he didn't there were plenty of other foreign students looking for work, she reminded herself stoically.

She went and sat down in a corner of the hotel lobby, not exactly hiding herself away out of sight, but certainly not making herself very obvious either, she recognised with a small stab of irritated despair. Why was she so lacking in confidence, so insecure, so…so vulnerable? It was not as though she had any reason to be. She was part of a very loving and closely knit family; she had parents who had always supported and protected her. Perhaps that was what it was. Perhaps they had protected her a little too much, she decided ruefully. Certainly Kelly, her friend, seemed to think so.

'The waiter couldn't remember what you'd ordered, so I've brought you a cappuccino…'

Beth nearly jumped out of her skin as she heard Alex's husky, sensual voice.

How had he found her here in this quiet corner? And, more importantly, how had he known she'd ordered coffee in the first place? And then, as he placed the tray he was carrying down on the table in front of her, Beth guessed what he had done. There were two cups of coffee on it and a croissant. No doubt all of them charged to her room!

'I actually ordered my coffee black,' she told him curtly, and not quite truthfully.

'Oh.' He gave her an oblique, smiling look. 'That's odd; I could have sworn you were a cappuccino girl. In fact I can almost see you with just a hint of a creamy chocolatey moustache.'

Beth stared at him in angry disbelief. He was taking far too many liberties, behaving far too personally. She gave him a ferociously frosty look and informed him arctically, 'As a woman, I hardly find that a flattering allusion. *Men* have moustaches.'

'Not the kind I mean,' he returned promptly as he sat down beside her, a wicked smile dancing in his eyes as he leaned forward. His lips were so close to her ear that she could actually feel the warmth of his breath as he whispered provocatively, 'The kind I meant is kissed off, not shaved…'

Beth's eyes widened in outraged fury.

He was actually pretending to flirt with her, pretending to find her *attractive*.

She started to get up, too furious to even bother telling him that she was not going to need his services, when, out of the corner of her eye, she caught sight of the beautiful crystal lustres the salesgirl was placing on the display shelves of the hotel's gift shop. Beth caught her breath. They were just so beautiful. The lustres moved gently, catching the light, their delicacy and beauty so immediately covetable that Beth ached to buy them.

A friend of her mother's had some antique Venetian ones which she had inherited from her grandmother, and Beth had always loved them.

'What is it?' she heard Alex asking her curiously at her side.

'The lustres...the wall-lights,' Beth explained. 'They're so beautiful.'

'Very beautiful and I'm afraid very expensive,' Alex told her. 'Were you thinking of buying them as a gift, or for yourself?'

'For my shop,' Beth told him absently, her attention concentrated on the lustres.

'You own a shop? Where? What kind?' His voice was less soft now, sharp with interest and something which Beth told herself was almost avaricious—too avaricious to be mere polite curiosity.

'Yes. I do...in a small town you won't have heard of. It's called Rye-on-Averton. I...we sell good-quality china and pottery ornaments and glassware. That's why I've come to Prague. I'm looking for new suppliers here, but the quality has to be right, and the price...'

'Well, you won't beat those pieces for quality,' Alex told her positively.

Beth looked at him, but before she could say anything he was telling her, 'Your coffee's going cold. You had better drink it and I had better introduce myself to you properly. As you know, I'm Alex Andrews.'

He held out his hand. A little reluctantly Beth took it. She had no idea why she felt so reluctant to touch him, or to have any kind of physical contact with him. Any other woman would have been more than eager to do so, she was quite sure. So what did that make her? A frightened little rabbit…too scared to touch such a good-looking and sexy man because she was afraid of the effect he might have on her? Of course not.

Quickly she shook his hand, and just as quickly released it, uncomfortably aware of the way her pulse-rate had quickened and her face become flushed.

'Beth Russell,' she responded.

'Yes, I know,' Alex told her, confessing, 'I asked them on Reception. What's it short for?'

'Bethany,' Beth told him.

'Bethany…I like that; it suits you. My grand-mother was a Beth as well. Her actual name was Alžběta, which she anglicised when she and my grandfather fled to Britain. She died before I was born—of a broken heart, my grandfather used to say, mourning the country and the family she had to leave behind.

'When my parents finally visited Prague, after the Revolution, my mother said that she found it incred-ibly moving to hear her family talking about her. She said it made her mother come alive for her. She died when my mother was eight…'

Beth made an involuntary sound of distress.

'Yes,' Alex agreed, confirming that he had heard and understood it. 'I feel the same way too. My mother missed out on so much—the loving presence of her mother *and* the comfort of being part of the large, extended family which she would have known had she grown up here in Prague. But then, of course, as my grandfather used to say, the opposite and darker side of that was the fact that because of his political beliefs he would have been persecuted and maybe even killed.

'The rest of the family certainly didn't escape unscathed. My grandfather was a younger son. His eldest brother would, in the normal course of events, have inherited both lands and a title from his father, but the Regime took all that away from the family.

'Now, of course, it has been restored. There are some families living in the Czech Republic today who have regained so many draughty castles that they're at a loss to know what to do with them all.

'Fortunately, in the case of my family, there is only the one. I shall take you to see it. It is very beautiful, but not so beautiful as you.'

Beth stared at him, completely lost for words. British he might claim to be, British his passport might *declare* him to be, but there was quite obviously a very strong Czech streak in him. Beth had done her homework before coming to Prague; she knew how the Czech people prided themselves on being artistic and sensitive, great poets and writers, idealists and romantics. Alex was certainly romantic. At least in the sense that he obviously enjoyed embroidering reality and the truth. There was no way *she* came anywhere near deserving to be described as beautiful, and it infuriated her that he should think her stupid enough to believe that she might be. Why was he doing it?

She was about to ask him when the lustres caught her eye again. Alex was right; they would be expensive on sale in a hotel like this one, but there must be other factories that made the same kind of thing—factories that did not charge expensive hotel prices to tourists. Without an interpreter, though, she would have no chance of finding them.

Beth turned to Alex Andrews.

'I know exactly what the going rate for interpreters is,' she warned him fiercely, 'and you will have to be able to drive. *And* I intend to check that the hotel management is prepared to vouch for you...'

The smile he was giving her was doing crazy things to her heart, making it flip over and then flop heavily against her chest wall like a stranded salmon.

'What are you *doing*?' she protested, panicking as Alex reached for her hand.

'Sealing our bargain with a kiss,' he told her softly as he lifted her nerveless fingers to his lips. And then, before they got there, he stopped and told her thoughtfully, 'Although perhaps on second thought...'

Beth went limp with relief. But it was a relief that came a little bit too soon, for, as she started to pull away, Alex leaned closer to her and swiftly captured her mouth with his own, kissing it firmly.

Beth was too shocked to move.

'You...you kissed me,' she gasped in a squeaky voice. 'But...'

'I've been wanting to do that from the first moment I saw you,' Alex told her huskily.

Beth stared at him.

Common sense, not to mention a sense of self-preservation, screamed to her that there was no way she could employ him as her interpreter, not after what he had just done, but his mesmeric grey eyes were hypnotising her, making it impossible for her to say what she knew ought to be said.

'We'll need a hire car,' he was telling her, just as though what he had done was the most natural thing in the world. 'I'll organise one.'

CHAPTER THREE

BETH gave a small sigh as she replaced the lustres on the glass shelves of the hotel's gift shop.

The previous day, after Alex Andrews had dropped her off following their visit to the first of the factories on her list, she had come into the shop and asked the price of the lustres they had on display.

As she had expected, they were expensive—*very* expensive.

'This piece is from one of our foremost crystal factories,' the salesgirl had explained to Beth. 'The lady whose family owns and runs the factory would never normally allow their things to be displayed in such a way, but she is a friend of the owner of the hotel. Normally they work only to order. Those wishing to buy their glassware have to visit the factory and speak with the people there themselves. The factory has been with the family for many, many generations, although it was taken away from them for a time during the Regime...'

'The lustre is very beautiful,' Beth had sighed.

Yes, it *was* very beautiful, she thought now as she left the gift shop.

The factories she had already visited today produced nothing even approaching the quality of the piece in the gift shop. The people she had met there had been friendly and helpful, eager to do business with her, but Beth had known the moment she saw their glassware range that it was not right for her shop—they specialised in highly individual pieces, highly covetable pieces. But it had not been her disappointment over the quality of what she had seen that had caused her to storm back to the car several paces ahead of Alex Andrews, her lips pressed together in a tight, angry line.

Still, at least this evening she would be seeing the stall holder in Wenceslas Square, who had promised her that she would bring her samples of the kind of glass she wanted to buy.

Yesterday, after Alex Andrews had left her to go and organise a hire car, Beth had spent an anxious hour restlessly walking by the river, trying to convince herself that she had not been as reckless as she feared in accepting his offer of help. For some reason, although technically she was the more senior 'partner' in their 'relationship', and she therefore held the power, the control, she couldn't quite escape the feeling that Alex had manoeuvred her into employing him, and that he was deliberately trying to manipulate her.

She'd known that she was going to have to be on her guard with him, and that she couldn't trust him. He was a man, after all, just like Julian. Another charmer…another chancer…

By the time he had returned she had told herself that she was fully armoured against him.

She'd deliberately had her lunch early, so that he wouldn't suggest they could eat together, thus ensuring that she wouldn't be tricked into paying for his meal. But even then he had *nearly* caught her out.

Eating so early had meant that she hadn't been particularly hungry, and so she had left the hotel dining room having barely touched her meal. Just as she had done so, Alex had walked into the hotel foyer. The warmth of the smile he had given her could quite easily have turned another woman's head, and Beth had certainly been conscious of the envious looks she'd attracted from the three female tourists who'd been watching them.

'We still haven't discussed exactly what you want to do,' Alex told her as he reached her. 'I thought we would have lunch together so that we can do so. There's a very good traditional restaurant not far from here that I know you'd enjoy...'

What she would not give for just one tenth of his impressive self-confidence, Beth thought enviously as she started to tell him curtly, 'No, I've already...'

'And these are the factories you want to visit,' Alex was saying as he picked up her list.

'Yes,' she agreed tersely.

'Mmm... Well, they certainly produce reasonable-quality crystal, but if what you're looking for is more along the lines of the pieces you were looking at in the gift shop then I would recommend...'

Alarm bells began to ring in Beth's brain. She had been warned at home to be wary of the touts paid by some of the more dubious manufacturers whose aim was to sell inferior-quality goods to the unwary at inflated prices.

'None of the reputable manufacturers would want to tarnish their reputations by becoming involved in that sort of thing,' she'd been told by a friend. 'The Czechs are a very artistic and a very proud people, but unfortunately, like any other nation, they have their less honest citizens. But that shouldn't affect you.'

'I don't want or need your recommendations, thank you,' she interrupted Alex abruptly. 'I am paying you to act as an interpreter and a driver. Whilst you were gone I've been looking at my maps. Since we're already halfway through the day, I think that today we should visit the closest of the factories, which will be this one here...'

As she spoke Beth held out the map to show him where she meant.

Immediately he began to frown.

'I wouldn't advise that you visit that particular factory,' he told her quietly. 'And as for it being the closest... As the crow flies, it may indeed seem so, but it can only be reached by a very circuitous route, and some recent storms in the area have resulted in heavy floods which have left some of the roads virtually impassable. And besides, I rather think if we did go there you'd be disappointed in what they produce.'

Beth could scarcely believe her ears. She had anticipated that she might have problems with him, and quite definitely had serious doubts about the wisdom of employing him, but she had scarcely expected him to start arguing with her right from the word go. His previous manner towards her had suggested quite the opposite, and it came as rather a shock to her to see him in such a decisive and, yes, dominant role. Where were the compliments he had given her earlier? Where was the easy charm and teasing warmth?

'I hadn't realised you were such an expert on crystal,' she told him tightly.

He gave a brief shrug and told her lightly, 'I should be; it's in the blood.'

Beth was slightly confused. What did he mean?

That because he was half-Czech he must automatically know about crystal? For sheer effrontery he had to be without equal, she decided angrily.

'Well, it may not be in *my* blood, but so far as I'm concerned I am still the best judge of what will and won't sell in *my* shop,' she told him assertively. 'And the only way I can decide whether or not any manufacturer produces the quality of crystal I want to sell is by seeing it for myself...'

'It's certainly one way of doing it,' Alex agreed. 'But you have to remember that the Czech Republic manufactures a very wide range of glass to suit all pockets and all tastes, and therefore, to my mind at least, it makes sense to eliminate those factories and manufacturers which are not going...which do not produce the type of goods you want.'

'Yes, it does,' Beth concurred, gritting her teeth as she told him, 'Which is why I was very specific about my requirements when I discussed them with our local Board of Trade representative before I left.'

'Perhaps you weren't specific enough,' Alex told her challengingly. 'Certainly, from my knowledge of them, at least half the factories on your list make either novelty or everyday glassware of a type I doubt you would be interested in.'

'Oh? I see. And you would know about that, of course. Tell me, Alex, don't you think it's rather stretching the arm of coincidence a little too far that miraculously, just as I should need an interpreter and guide, one turns up who purports to be an expert not just in the manufacture of crystal but also in knowing exactly what type of goods I want?'

There was a brief pause before Alex responded with unexpected dryness, 'Not really. After all, crys-

tal is one of the country's most famous exports.
Naturally I suspect that any guide you would have
employed would have known something about its
manufacture...'

'But not so much as you?' Beth suggested cynically.

'No, not so much as me,' he agreed gravely. 'But
I can see that you're determined not to take my advice and so...' he glanced at his watch '...the sooner
we leave the better, if you really want to visit this
specific factory this afternoon.'

Later, as they drove in an uncomfortable silence over
roads which Beth was forced to acknowledge were
not the best she had ever ridden on, she admitted
inwardly to herself that had it been another guide, an
accredited guide, who had suggested to her that she
might find it more difficult to reach her destination
than she had envisaged she would probably have listened and accepted such advice, but because it had
been Alex...

But then, hadn't she every reason to suspect him?
she asked herself defensively. Look at the way he
had introduced himself to her and flirted with her.
Not that he was flirting with her *now*... Far from it.
She glanced briefly at him as he sat beside her, con-
centrating on his driving.

Even dressed in a pair of faded jeans and a polo
shirt he still possessed a very powerful presence, a
very potent maleness, she acknowledged reluctantly.

It was plain, too, that she had offended him earlier
by rejecting his advice—his *unwanted* advice, she
reminded herself—because there was quite definitely
a very stern and remote set to his mouth. And, whilst

he had been polite, and careful to describe to her the historical nature of the countryside they had been driving through, he had done so in a way that had very definitely kept a distance between them. Which, of course, was exactly what she had wanted—wasn't it? Of course it was. She was simply not the sort of person, the sort of *woman*, who got any sort of pleasure or…or…anything else out of challenging people and creating an atmosphere of tension and sexual aggression between herself and a man. No, she didn't find that sort of thing exciting or…or stimulating in any possible kind of way.

It turned out that the factory which was their destination could only be reached by a cobbled road with a teeth-jarringly uneven camber, so much so that when they finally drew up in front of it Beth had to stop herself from exhaling a pent-up breath of relief.

It would never do to allow Alex Andrews to think that she regretted not listening to his advice, but cravenly, as they started to walk towards the factory, Beth prayed that the glassware she had come to see would vindicate her decision and make their trip worthwhile.

Picturesquely the factory was housed in what seemed an almost fortress-like building-cum-castle, but when Beth couldn't help remarking on this Alex told her grimly, 'Until recently it was used as a prison.'

A prison. Beth shivered and took a few steps backwards just at the moment when a dilapidated lorry came roaring into the small courtyard.

She heard the screech of its brakes as its driver reacted to her presence but for some reason she found it impossible to move, even though she could see the lorry bearing down on her.

A few feet away from her she heard Alex curse as he moved like lightning, turning and grabbing hold of her, lifting her bodily off her feet as he swung her out of the lorry's path.

The whole incident had lasted less than a handful of seconds but it left Beth badly shaken. So much so that she could actually feel herself trembling violently as Alex continued to hold her.

'It's all right…it's all right,' she could hear him saying gruffly to her. 'You're safe…'

Safe!

Beth raised her head to look at him, the politely formal words of thanks she had intended to utter forgotten as her glance meshed with his.

How could eyes that were such a cool pale grey look so…so hot, like molten mercury?

'Alex…'

She could feel the heat in his gaze as it shifted from her eyes to her mouth. Her lips started to tremble—and soften. Involuntarily she could feel them starting to part…to open in an age-old signal of female recognition—and invitation.

This couldn't be happening, she told herself hazily. She *couldn't* be standing here in the courtyard of this dilapidated building knowing that Alex Andrews intended to kiss her, knowing it and not doing the slightest thing to prevent him from doing so other than to utter a token 'no' as the downward descent of his head blotted out the daylight and she felt the warm, sure pressure of his mouth against hers.

If she was completely honest, when Julian had kissed her she had never truly enjoyed the too wet, too soft sensation of his mouth on hers, and had, on many occasions, actively tried to avoid it.

Some women were just not particularly highly sexed, she had assured herself, and she quite obviously was one of them—which made it all the more extraordinary that she should feel, the moment Alex Andrews' mouth touched hers, as though her whole body was engulfed in a heat even greater than that generated by the blast furnaces used to heat silica.

Was it possible that somehow Alex Andrews had the power to convert her raw anger and dislike, her suspicion of him, into something else, a very different kind of emotion, just as the heat the furnaces used on the raw ingredients of the silica sand could turn it into the molten liquid which ultimately could be converted into the most beautiful crystal glass? But of course it wasn't. How could the negative, self-defensive emotions she felt towards Alex ever be converted into something else, especially since she herself didn't want them to be? So then why was she melting so into his arms, into his body; why was *her* body becoming molten liquid with the white heat of her own desire?

'Do you believe in love at first sight?' Alex asked hoarsely against her lips. His hands were cupping her face, his thumbs gently stroking the hot flesh of her flushed cheeks.

'Oh, yes,' Beth sighed mistily.

Hadn't it always been one of her most cherished private dreams that one day she would meet a man, *the* man, and from the very first second of setting eyes on him, she would just know that *he* was *the* one?

But of course that was a silly, almost adolescent

fantasy, a daydream that, now she was a grown woman, life and reality had forced her to abandon.

The mistiness in her eyes gave way to a grave sadness that told Alex far more than her silence and the abrupt, fierce denial which followed it.

'No. No, of *course* I don't. Love at first sight, it's a fiction, a fantasy,' Beth objected angrily. 'It's…it's *impossible*.'

'No, not impossible,' Alex corrected her gently. 'Incomprehensible from a logical point of view, perhaps, but not impossible. Ask any poet…'

'Oh, poets,' Beth denounced dismissively, but the sharp tone of her voice was still at odds with the betraying expression in her eyes.

Someone, somewhere in her past, had hurt her—and badly, Alex recognised. Someone at some time had robbed her of her faith and her trust, had forced her to retreat into the prickly thicket she had built around her emotions, but *he* could see what lay beyond that thicket; *he* could see in her eyes the woman that she actually was—a tender, loving, *lovable* woman, a woman who—

'Oh, no…look over there,' Beth commanded, her voice suddenly as filled with emotion as her eyes as she pointed in the direction where a cat was stalking an unaware bird.

'Oh, no. *No.* It's going to catch it…'

As he heard the urgency and the anxiety in her voice Alex reacted instinctively, clapping his hands loudly together to distract the cat and alert its potential victim.

As the bird flew away, and the cat gave him a baleful glare, Beth turned to him, her eyes shining with relief.

'Oh, that was good,' she praised him involuntarily. 'I'm glad you didn't hurt the cat, like some people might have done...I wouldn't have wanted it to be hurt. After all, it's only obeying nature...'

Such a soft, tender heart, Alex marvelled, but apparently there was no softness or tenderness in it for him...apparently... When he had kissed her her kisses had been honey-sweet, but the words she spoke to him were vinegar-sharp and they were not, he felt sure, the words of her heart.

How long was she going to be here in Prague?

Somehow he would find a way of persuading her to drop her guard and allow him into her life...her heart...her love... Somehow.

Seeing the look in his eyes, Beth went cold with the icy sweat of misery that swamped her. What was it about her that gave Alex the idea that she was so desperate to be loved, so vulnerable to his patently false flattery that she would be deceived by him? Did she really come across as so needy, so...so... helpless? How many times before had Alex used the same ploy on other gullible female tourists? Beth's teeth started to chatter, the icy cold shivers racking her nothing to do with the cool mountain air. In Prague it had been a warm, sunny day when they had left, but here it was much cooler, the sun obscured by mist.

'You're cold,' Alex was telling her. 'Here, take this...'

Before she could stop him he was removing his own jacket and wrapping it around her.

She wanted to refuse. The jacket smelled tormentingly of him, a subtle, sensually male scent that she could have sworn she would not normally have noticed, but which for some reason she suddenly seemed to have become acutely responsive to—far too acutely—if the heat that was now flooding her body was anything to go by.

Quickly she moved away from Alex and deliberately removed the notebook she had brought with her from her handbag. According to the details she had been given at home, the factory they were about to visit produced an extensive range of modestly priced goods.

What she was looking for, in addition to the kind of crystal she could sell in the shop, were some artistic and unusual little pieces that would make an eye-catching window display and tempt people in to buy, something along the lines of the pretty, delicately tinted glass sweets she had seen displayed to good effect in an exclusive shop she had once visited in the Cotswolds.

With one eye on the Christmas market, Beth was thinking in terms of some pretty and delicate glass Christmas tree ornaments, or even possibly some novelty, but still attractive, glass swizzle sticks.

However, once they had presented themselves in the factory's main office, and she had introduced herself to the factory manager, Beth's heart started to sink as he proceeded to show her some samples of the type of article they made.

The manager's English was good enough for her not to have needed the services of an interpreter, which, when she realised that all Alex's warnings about the unsuitability of the factory's goods for her market had been more than justified, made her chagrin increase.

The things she was being shown were simply not

of the high standard required by her customers, and
far too mass market for her one-off select gift shop.
With a heavy heart Beth wondered how on earth she
was going to get out of accepting the offer of a tour
of the factory which the manager was enthusiastically offering her. She had no wish to hurt his feelings, but...

Behind her she could hear Alex saying something
to the factory manager in Czech. Enquiringly she
looked at him.

'I was just explaining to him that since you have
other factories to visit there won't be time for you to
accept his very kind offer,' Alex told her smoothly.

Illogically, instead of feeling grateful to him for
his timely rescue, Beth discovered as they headed
back to the car that what she was actually experiencing was a seething, impotent, smouldering, re-
sentful anger.

'Is something wrong?' Alex asked her in what she
knew had to be pseudo-concern as he unlocked the
passenger door of the car for her.

'You could say that,' Beth snapped acidly back at
him in response. 'In future, I'd prefer it if you allowed me to make my *own* decisions instead of making them for me.'

As she spoke she wrenched impatiently at the car
door handle, and then gave a small, involuntary yelp
of frustrated anger when it refused to yield.

Imperturbably Alex reached past her and opened
it for her.

'And will you please stop treating me as though
I'm totally incapable of doing anything for myself?'
Beth told him sharply.

'I'm sorry if I'm offending you, but I was brought

up in the old-fashioned way—where good manners were important and where it was expected that a man should exhibit them.'

'Yes, I can see that. I suppose your mother stayed at home and obeyed your father's every whim…'

Beth knew even as she spoke that what she was saying was unforgivably rude. No matter what her personal opinion was of men who treated women as second-class citizens, she still had no right to criticise Alex's home life. Alex, though, far from being offended, was actually throwing back his head and laughing, a warm, unfettered sound of obvious amusement which strangely, instead of reassuring her, made her feel even more angry than before.

'I'm sorry,' he apologised. 'I shouldn't laugh, but if you knew my mother—*when* you get to know my mother,' he amended with a very meaningful look, 'you'll understand why I did. My mother is a highly qualified senior consultant, specialising in heart disorders. She worked all through my childhood and still continues to do so. The old-fashioned influence in my life actually came from my grandfather, who lived with us.'

Immediately Beth felt remorseful and ashamed. Her own grandparents, who lived in the same small Cornish village as her parents, were similarly old-fashioned and insistent on the necessity of good manners.

'I apologise if you thought I was trying to patronise you,' Alex added once they were both in the car. 'That certainly wasn't my intention.' He paused and looked straight at her, and then told her softly, 'Has anyone ever told you that you have the most sexily kissable mouth? Especially when you're trying hard not to smile…'

Beth gave him a frosty look.

'I'd really prefer it if you didn't try to flirt with me,' she told him primly.

She tried to look away, but discovered that she couldn't; there was something dangerously and powerfully mesmeric about the intent look in Alex's eyes.

'What makes you think I'm flirting?' he challenged her silkily. 'And don't try to pretend to me that you aren't just as aware of what's happening between us as I am…I felt it in the way you reacted when I kissed you…'

Reduced to a mortified, tongue-tied silence, Beth could only manage to turn away from him and drag her gaze from his.

He was certainly persistent; she had to give him that. Personally, she didn't know why he was bothering. She must have made it plain to him by now that she was no push-over, and that his dubious talents could be put to far more profitable use on another and more gullible female tourist.

It was tempting to tell him just why she was so immune to his practised flattery, but to do so would undoubtedly involve her in some more of the kind of dialogue at which, she was beginning to discover, he was more adept than she—and there was no way she was going to allow him to get the upper hand in their 'relationship' again.

CHAPTER FOUR

'HAVE you made any plans for this evening?'

Beth tensed as she listened to Alex's question. They had just walked into the hotel foyer, following their abortive visit to the factory. The journey had left her feeling tired and a little stiff, and she was looking forward to having a hot bath and an early night—on her own.

'I've got some paperwork I need to deal with,' she answered quickly, and not entirely untruthfully. Well, she did have some postcards she could write, and then she wanted to make a few notes on the factory she had visited and to read up on those she still had to see.

'I would have asked you to join me for dinner,' Alex continued, 'only I'm already committed this evening—a family celebration; we're going to the opera and—'

'I hope you enjoy it,' Beth told him politely, wondering why, when by rights she ought to have been both relieved and pleased to learn that she was not going to be pressured into spending the evening with him, what she actually felt was an uncomfortable and indigestible sense of abandonment and disappointment.

'Do you?' Alex challenged her gently, stepping forward as he did so.

Panicking that he might be going to kiss her again, Beth immediately stepped back from him, and then saw from the amused twinkle in his eyes that he had realised what she was thinking.

'You're safe here,' he told her teasingly. 'It's far, far too public for what *I've* got in mind.'

The lift doors opened, disgorging half a dozen hotel guests, and Alex nodded towards them, telling her softly, 'Now, had we been in *there* it might have been a different thing. There's something very, very erotic about the thought of making love, wanting one another so much that it's impossible to wait until one reaches the security of one's room—of *needing* one another so immediately that one's prepared to take the risk of being discovered, of having one's passionate surge towards fulfilment interrupted...'

Beth stared at him, her face starting to flush, her body hot with reaction to the soft sensuality of his slowly spoken words and to the mental images he was conjuring up in her own suddenly fevered imagination.

'I wouldn't know. I do not have those kind of thoughts,' she told him distancingly and defensively.

For the second time that day Alex threw back his head and laughed.

'Somehow I don't believe you,' he told her wickedly. 'I think that in secret, in private, *you* are a very sexy, very sensual woman indeed. But you prefer to keep the secret, the sweetness of that sensuality hidden from all but your chosen lover. And who can blame you for that? Or him for wanting to explore that private sweetness and possess it...possess you...?'

Beth didn't know what to say or do. The way he was behaving—the things he was saying, the intimacy he was creating between them—was so totally outside her own experience that she simply didn't know how to deal with it.

'What time do you want me?' Alex was asking her huskily. Beth stared at him, involuntarily licking her suddenly dry lips. 'After breakfast...about nine?' he was adding.

He meant what time did she want him to meet her in the morning, Beth realised. For one moment she had actually thought...

After Beth had left him Alex did not leave the hotel straight away. Instead he walked over to the gift shop, thoughtfully studying the lustres that Beth had admired.

In some ways the glass reminded him of Beth. Like her it was delicate, and yet surprisingly resilient. Like her its purity and beauty made one catch one's breath, inspired and moved the human soul. Beth certainly inspired and moved his soul, not to mention certain far less ethereal parts of his body, he reflected ruefully. He had never known himself to be so dangerously at the mercy of his own emotions.

Perhaps it had something to do with the fact that he was in Prague. Perhaps being here released a hitherto unsuspected and very deeply emotional part of his personality, enabled him, empowered him to react instinctively and immediately to those emotions instead of behaving with caution and logic as he would have done at home. Classic symptoms of a holiday romance? Alex grimaced to himself. In many ways he wished that were the case, but he knew himself too well to accept such a definition of his feelings.

Love at first sight.

How did you account for the unexpectedness of such feelings? How did you evaluate or analyse

them? You couldn't…you simply had to acknowledge that they were too strong, too powerful, too
overwhelming for mere mortal logic to deal with.

Beth.

Bethany…

Alex closed his eyes, trying to blot out how the
sound of her name as it left his lips would make a
possessive male litany of love and desire against her
skin as he held and caressed her. In the morning light
her skin would be as flawless and perfect as the crystal teardrops on the lustres.

No. This was no mere holiday romance, no mere
giving in to the mood and magic of the city, even if
Prague was a city that was a part of his heritage and
his blood. Perhaps the intensity, the impetuosity driving him on now was a previously unfamiliar part of
the British side of his personality.

Perhaps if he was honest he was a little bemused
by what was happening to him. Bemused, but still
instinctively and automatically convinced that his
love was the love of his lifetime, a love that would
last a lifetime.

Convincing Beth, though, he suspected, was not
going to be easy. She was suspicious of him, and
perhaps rightly so, and he could see, oh, so clearly,
how much her outward antagonism towards him, her
animosity, masked an inner fragility and fear.
Somehow he would find a way to show her that she
had no need of those protective barriers against him.
Somehow he would find a way…

After Alex had gone—unexpectedly without asking
her to pay him for the day—Beth went upstairs to
her room, intending to spend the rest of the evening

there. But once she had bathed and eaten she suddenly got an unexpected surge of energy. From her bedroom window she had an excellent view of the river. The sky had cleared and was now washed with a tempting evening palette of colours; soft blue, pale yellow and a heavenly indescribable silvery pink.

Down below her in the square she could see people strolling around, or sitting at the pavement cafés.

She was, she reminded herself, here to enjoy herself, and to explore Prague and its historical beauty, as well as on a buying trip.

Before she could change her mind she dressed in comfortably casual chinos and a soft shirt and, picking up her jacket and bag, made her way down to the hotel foyer.

Her guidebook had an excellent street map; she could hardly get lost. Wenceslas Square was her ultimate destination. It featured largely in all the articles she had read about the city and, to judge from the photographs, with good reason.

As she walked in the Square's direction her attention was distracted by the plethora of shops selling crystal and china. At each one she stopped to examine the contents of their windows. All of the goods displayed were breathtakingly good value, but, to her disappointment, none of them had on show the same quality of glass she had seen in the hotel gift shop. She was just re-examining the display in one window when a young man approached her.

Only eighteen or so, he gave her a winning smile and introduced himself in broken English, asking her if she would like a guide to show her the city.

Firmly Beth refused, relieved when he immediately accepted her refusal and walked away. The

Square was only a few yards away now, right at the end of the street she was on, but even though she had seen the photographs, and read the enthusiastic descriptive guide to it, she was still not totally prepared for its magnificence, nor for the sense of stepping back into history that walking into it gave her.

Here, surrounded by the stall holders displaying their wares, it was almost possible to feel that she had stepped back into the medieval age... A juggler juggling brightly painted balls winked at her as she walked past him; in the centre of the Square a quartet were vigorously playing classical music. A little boy clung nervously to his mother as a fire-eater leant backwards to swallow the licking flames of fire he was holding. A few feet away acrobats tumbled, reminding Beth that the Czech Republic was famed for its highly skilled circus acts.

But it was the stalls that gripped her real attention, taking her back to her childhood and the wonder of visiting antiques fairs with her grandparents. Here it was once again possible to capture that age-old magic. At one stall a man was actually making sets of armour as his customers waited. At another a dark gypsy woman was displaying hand-made jewellery. But it was the stalls selling glassware that predictably drew Beth like a magnet.

Slowly she wandered from one to another, trying not to feel too desperately disappointed when she realised that there was nothing for her to buy.

'You are looking for something special?' one stall holder asked her encouragingly. 'A gift, perhaps...?'

Beth shook her head.

'No. No, not a gift,' she told her. 'Actually, I'm

here on business. I have a shop at home in England and I want...'

She paused, not sure just why she was confiding in this dark-eyed gypsy woman with her insistent manner.

'I have seen a piece of glass in the gift shop of my hotel—very Venetian...baroque, crimson, painted...gilded...'

'Ah, yes, I know just what you mean,' the woman told her enthusiastically. 'We do not sell such pieces here, but I know where to get them. If you would be interested in seeing some I could get some for you to look at, say for this time tomorrow...'

Beth stared at her, hardly daring to believe her luck.

'Are you sure we're talking about the same thing?' she began doubtfully. 'All the glass I have seen so far...'

'Is like this. No...' The woman finished for her, rummaging in a large box and triumphantly producing a book which she handed to Beth.

Beth stared at the photograph the woman was showing her, scarcely able to contain her excitement. The goblets depicted in it were exactly what she was looking for: heavy, antique, made in richly coloured glass.

'Yes...yes, that's *exactly* what I want,' she agreed.

But Beth was no fool.

'But these here in this photograph are genuine antiques,' she felt bound to point out.

'These are, yes,' the woman agreed after a small pause. 'However, there is a factory where they specialise in making such glass—but only to special orders, you understand.'

Special orders. Beth looked doubtfully at her, re-membering the price she had been quoted for the lustre in the gift shop.

'But surely that means they will be very expen-sive…'

'Maybe…maybe not,' the woman replied myste-riously. 'It all depends on the size of the order, no? I shall bring some for you to see,' she announced, closing the book. 'If you will be here at this time tomorrow evening I shall show you what a good bar-gain we can make…'

Half an hour later, as she hurried back to the hotel, Beth asked herself what she had to lose by returning to the stall tomorrow evening.

Nothing…

After all, she hadn't made any kind of commit-ment to buy anything. She was simply going to look, that was all.

Caught up in her excitement, she suddenly realised that she had lost her way a little, and that she was now in a part of the city that was unfamiliar to her. There was an imposing building in front of her which she was sure must feature in her guidebook. All she had to do was to check the name of the square she was now in and redirect herself to her hotel.

As she delved into her bag for her guidebook a large crowd of people suddenly started to emerge from the building she had been studying, all of them dressed in evening clothes. Idly watching them, Beth suddenly froze as she recognised Alex Andrews amongst them. If he had looked toughly masculine earlier in the day, dressed in jeans and a polo shirt, that was nothing to the way he looked now, wearing a dinner suit. Taller than most of the other men in the crowd, he would have stood out even without his strikingly handsome good looks, simply on account of the way he held himself, Beth recognised.

As Beth watched him she suddenly realised that not only was he not alone but that the woman who was with him was the same soignée, elegant older woman she had seen him talking with in the hotel foyer the previous day.

Alex was patently oblivious to *her* presence, and as Beth observed them from the shadows she saw him put a very protective arm around the older woman whilst she, in turn, moved closer to him, lifting her face towards his with such a luminous look of love in her expression that Beth felt her throat start to close up and she was swamped by a mixture of contempt and anger. So much for his comments to *her*. It was quite plain that his companion believed that she had a *very* special and intimate relationship with him. Beth only had to witness the way he lifted her hand to his face, gently touching his cheek, to see that.

Her stomach churned with nauseating disgust. Not for the older woman, who plainly believed that Alex returned the feelings Beth could see so clearly revealed on her face, but for Alex, who quite obviously had no compunction whatsoever about what he was doing.

So much for the family gathering he had told her he was attending. But why was she so shocked—and so upset? Surely what she had just witnessed only confirmed what she already knew—that, quite simply, he was not to be trusted. Instead of feeling this helpless, anguished sense of loss and betrayal, she

ought to be feeling pleased that her suspicions were
vindicated.

She *was* pleased that they had been vindicated,
Beth assured herself doggedly. She was more than
pleased—she was delighted. *Delighted.*

'Have you seen the Charles Bridge yet?'

Beth shook her head, not wanting to allow Alex
to engage her in any unnecessary conversation. After
what she had seen last night she had made herself a
vow that she would make it plain to him that there
was no way she was going to fall for his cynical
manipulation of her feelings.

In fact just as soon as she had had her breakfast
she had approached the hotel manager to ask if there
was any chance that another interpreter might now
be free, but once again she had met with the same
response. The conventions taking place in the city
meant that it was impossible for them to provide her
with this service.

Tempted though Beth had been to tell Alex that
she simply no longer required his help, common
sense had forced her to acknowledge that this would
be cutting off her nose to spite her face. Although it
was true that most Czechs could either speak or understand English, Beth needed to be very sure of exactly what was being said if she should decide to
give any of the factories an order, and she also
needed someone to help her negotiate the best possible price she could for whatever she might decide
to order, and that meant having someone with her
who had a proper grasp of the Czech language.

However, there was one thing she could do, and
that was make sure that she spent as little time as

possible with Alex Andrews, and to that end Beth had decided that today, instead of only visiting two factories, she would insist that they manage to visit three, which meant that would leave her with only another half a dozen on her list.

'No? Then *I* shall take you to see it,' Alex was announcing, ignoring Beth's steely silence. 'I expect you already know that it was the first permanent bridge to be built in Northern Europe and—'

'Yes, I *have* read the guidebooks,' Beth interrupted him shortly. 'But as for seeing it…' She shook her head and told him briskly, 'I'm here on business, and that has to take priority over everything else…'

As she spoke she couldn't resist looking towards the gift shop. The lustres were still there, tantalisingly.

She gave a sigh.

'I have been thinking,' Alex told her quietly. 'If good-quality reproduction Venetian baroque crystal *is* what you are looking for then my cousins' factory is most definitely somewhere you should visit. If you should wish to visit I'm sure I could arrange something.'

'Yes, I'm sure you could,' Beth agreed sarcastically. Just how stupid did he think she was?

'Is your cousins' factory mentioned on my list?' she asked him, already knowing what the answer would be.

As she had known he would, Alex shook his head as she held her list out to him.

'These factories were originally state-owned, and though they are now back in private hands they do not… My cousins' factory is not like them. It does not cater to the mass market. Until the Revolution they mainly supplied the Russian hierarchy.'

'Fascinating though the history of your family undoubtedly is—to you,' she told him coolly, 'I'm afraid that I simply don't have time to listen to it.' She glanced at her watch. 'There are three factories I want to see today, so I suggest that we make a start...'

She could see that Alex was starting to frown.

'Beth,' he began, reaching out to catch hold of her arm. Unable to move in time to prevent him, Beth went rigid as she felt his fingers circle her wrist.

'What is it? What's wrong?' he asked her huskily. His thumb was resting on the pulse in her wrist and she could feel it starting to hammer frantically against his touch. He could obviously feel it as well, because his thumb started to move against her skin in a rhythmic, circular stroking movement that should have been soothing but for some reason had quite the opposite effect on her hypersensitive nervous system.

'Nothing's wrong,' she lied jerkily, willing herself not to allow the deep tremor she could feel beginning deep within her body like some subterranean force to manifest itself in open shivers and shudders of reaction.

And then, to her own self-contempt, she heard herself asking him sharply, 'Did you enjoy yourself last night—with your family?'

The appraising look he gave her made her wish she had kept silent.

'Yes, I did,' he agreed calmly, 'but nowhere near so much as I would have had you been with us, and certainly nowhere near so much as I would had we been alone…'

Beth's gasp was, she assured herself, one of furious female outrage. How dared he have the barefaced cheek to stand there and say such a thing to her when she knew, when she had seen with her own eyes, just how he had spent his evening and with whom?

'Tonight, I want you to have dinner with me,' he was continuing. 'Tonight, I want you,' he added, underlining the sensuality of his message and his desire.

But that desire was faked, flawed, a lie, and Beth knew it.

'I can't. I've already made arrangements for this evening,' she told him coolly.

Ridiculous to feel that *she* was at fault just because of the way he managed to fake those dark shadows in his eyes and that male look of hurt withdrawal in the tightness of his mouth. *She* was the one who was being badly treated, not him.

'You're not going to find what you're looking for at any of the factories on your list,' Alex informed Beth as they left the third factory.

'No. I'm coming to realise that,' Beth said testily. She felt both tired and disappointed, but that was not the real cause of her defensive anger and she knew it. Five hours of being cooped up in a small car with Alex was beginning to have its effect on her equilibrium—and her emotions.

She had done everything she could to hold him at a distance, but to her chagrin, instead of recognising that she had guessed what he was up to, he'd seemed to think that she wasn't very well, anxiously asking her in some concern several times if she was suffering from a headache or feeling unwell. Only her own cautious nature had prevented her from telling him that if she *was* suffering from any kind of malaise then he was its cause. But there was more to what she was experiencing than that, she was forced to acknowledge honestly.

Had she simply been able to feel for him the contempt and disdain she knew he deserved then there would have been no need for her defensive and protective anger. But against all logic, and certainly against any cerebral desire on her part, she was unable to deny her body's physical reaction, her body's physical *response* to him; that was why she was getting so uptight and angry.

Every time he made some comment about wanting her, every time he alluded to how much he desired her, she could feel herself starting to react to him. And she had even, at one morale-lowering point, found herself wishing that he *would* put his softly suggestive comment about longing to silence her sharp tongue with his mouth into action.

'You're so prickly that a man can't help but feel tempted to wonder what it would take to make you purr,' he'd informed her outrageously when she had refused his suggestion that they find somewhere to have lunch.

'You're right,' he had agreed, when she had told him shortly that she didn't want to eat, his eyes suddenly dark and hot. '*My* appetite isn't for food either. What I really want to taste is the sweet softness of your flesh. Its juices will be like nectar, honey to my lips, whilst—'

'Stop it,' Beth had demanded frantically, unable to screen out the mental images his erotic words had provoked for her. How could she dislike him so much, distrust him so much, and yet, at the same time, *want* him so much?

It was just sex, she told herself fiercely. That was all. For some reason he had aroused within her a hitherto unexperienced need, a desire she had never suspected herself capable of feeling. The hesitant and awkward experiments of her teenage years had simply not prepared her for what she was feeling now— and that was all it was, a quirky build-up of the sexual desire she should perhaps have felt at a younger age but which, for some reason, she had not, and which was now manifesting itself in this totally unacceptable reaction to Alex Andrews.

Yes, *that* was what it was, she decided in relief. It was just sex...just an itch that needed scratching... Shocked by the unfamiliar directness of her own thoughts, Beth tried to concentrate on the countryside they were driving through. Just because she now knew the cause of her disturbing reaction to Alex, that didn't mean she had to give in to it, she warned herself. And at least it meant she no longer had to worry about it, she told herself in relief.

'Look...I'm sorry if I seem to be crowding you or rushing you,' Alex was saying gruffly at her side. 'All this is new territory for me, you know. I've never actually felt like this before, experienced anything like this before. I always knew that one day I would fall in love just as passionately and permanently as my grandfather fell in love with my grandmother, but I have to confess I didn't expect it to be so...'

Heavens, but he was quick, clever... Beth acknowledged as she forced herself to be detached and step outside her own feelings to admire the adroit way he was handling not just the situation but her as well.

First the advance, now the back-off. No doubt he expected her to feel chagrin and to start pursuing *him*. And as for that schmaltzy comment about his grandparents…!

CHAPTER FIVE

'I'M SORRY that none of the factories we visited to-day came up to your expectations.' Alex joined her in the hotel's gift shop and looked at his watch. 'It's too late for me to organise anything now, but why don't I give my cousins a ring and arrange for you to visit their factory? We could...'

They moved back into the hotel foyer, which was very busy with business-suited people who Beth assumed must be attending one of the conferences in the hotel the manager had told her about. She felt tired and disappointed, but those feelings weren't the real cause of the desire she felt to snap sharply at Alex.

Why, when she knew exactly what kind of man he was and exactly what he was after, was she experiencing this sense of new panic and fear that her self-control might not prove strong enough for her to hold him at bay? What was the matter with her? Surely she had enough intelligence to know that once one had been struck by lightning a first time one did not return to the same tree in a thunderstorm and stand there waiting for it to happen again. Not unless one was a very peculiar sort of person who thrived on suffering pain.

Was she that kind of person, the kind of person who only attracted the sort of relationship, the sort of *man* who would hurt and humiliate her? Beth knew from the strength of her own inner abhorrence that she wasn't.

So why, then, did she feel the way she did?

She felt the way she did because she was sexually attracted to Alex, she told herself brutally; she was chemically and hormonally responsive to him. That was all... It crossed her mind as the movement of the crowd pushed her up against him and he reached out automatically to hold her that it might almost be worthwhile actually giving in to what she was feeling, what she was *wanting*, and simply having sex with him. Perhaps once she had done so, once he had realised that she was able to separate her feelings of sexual desire for him from her emotions, that just because she went to bed with him it didn't mean she was going to allow him to persuade her to give his cousins her business or him her money, he might stop trying to pressurise her. After all, she already knew that the only real interest he had in her was a financial one, despite the attention he was paying her and the compliments he was giving her.

'It's too crowded in here. We could talk more easily in your room.'

Alex's words, whispered so temptingly against her ear, mirroring so closely the intimate sensuality of her own thoughts, threw Beth into feminine panic.

'No. No...' she denied quickly, frantically trying to make some space between them. Could Alex feel the tumultuous, uneven thudding of her heartbeat as clearly as she could feel the deep male pounding of his? And, if he could, was it having the same intense effect upon his senses as his was upon hers? Beth closed her eyes, struggling to break free of the tide of hungry need she could feel welling up inside her.

All day long she had been fighting against this; all day long she had been struggling to hold both Alex and her own unfamiliar responsiveness to him at bay.

Now, pressed up against him in the airless atmosphere of the hotel lobby, she was terrifyingly aware of how readily her senses responded to him, of how great the temptation was not to move away from him but to move *closer*.

'I could ring my cousins from your room,' Alex was telling her persuasively. 'I promise you you won't be disappointed, Beth.'

Was it just her imagination, or was he subtly implying that her expectations of pleasure would not merely be satisfied by the quality of his cousins' glass? Beth could feel her face starting to burn with hectic hormone-driven colour.

The warmth of his breath as he spoke to her was so tantalisingly like a caress that she had to grit her teeth to stop herself from moving closer to it, to stop herself from imagining how it would feel to have the soft caress of his mouth moving against the tender, vulnerable pleasure spot just behind her ear, to move from there to...

Beneath her clothes Beth could feel her nipples peaking and thrusting eagerly against their protective covering, flaunting their availability and their need.

Frantically Beth decided that she had to do something, anything, to put a stop to what was happening.

'From the way you're talking, anyone would think that your cousins are the *only* manufacturers who produce high-quality reproduction antique glass,' she told Alex challengingly, gritting her teeth as she deliberately pushed herself away from him and looked into his face.

'Well, they aren't the *only* ones, but they do have a reputation for being the best. Of the only other two I know, one has order books going right into the millennium—mainly from its American customers— and the other is presently in negotiation with an Italian company that wants to go into partnership with them.'

'How very convenient,' Beth told him sarcastically. 'But as it happens I've actually found my own source...'

'You have?' Alex was frowning slightly. 'May I ask where? None of the factories you've got listed...'

'It isn't somewhere on my list,' Beth told him, too infuriated by his patronising manner to be guarded or cautious. 'I've been told by one of the gypsy stall holders in Wenceslas Square that she can supply me with an introduction to a factory that makes the quality of glass I want.'

'A stall holder in the Square?' Alex looked patently unimpressed. 'And you believed her?' he derided, before asking her hardily, 'You didn't give her any money, did you?'

'No, I didn't. Not that it's any of your business,' Beth defended herself sharply. She felt like a naughty child, called up before her head teacher to explain herself, and it wasn't a sensation she was enjoying. What right, after all, did Alex have to question any of her decisions? And as for his comment about her not parting with any money...!

'She's going to get some samples of the glass for me to look at...'

'You've told her where you're staying?'

If anything he was looking even more disapproving, and a belated sense of caution warned Beth not to tell him that she had actually arranged to go down to the Square to meet with the stall holder that evening.

'She knows how to get in touch with me,' was all she permitted herself to say.

'You do know the reputations some of these gypsies have, don't you?' Alex demanded. 'You must have been warned. A lot of them are illegal immigrants into the country. They are well known to be in the pay of organised criminals…'

'What, *all* of them?' Beth derided him, parodying his tone of voice to her minutes earlier.

'This is not a situation you should take lightly,' Alex told her sternly. 'These are potentially very dangerous people.'

Beth couldn't help herself. Childish though she knew it was, she gave a heavy, theatrically bored sigh that stopped Alex speaking immediately and caused his mouth to harden into an implacably tight line.

'Very well,' he told her curtly. 'If you won't listen to my advice then at least, for your own safety and my peace of mind, let me be there when you see these people.'

Let him be there… Knowing what she did, and knowing now just how determined he was to push her in the direction of his family's business—no way.

The crowd which had thronged the lobby was thinning out now. The girl behind the reception desk, catching sight of Alex, signalled to him.

'Excuse me,' he said to Beth quickly, walking towards the desk. Beth could hear the girl saying something to him in Czech—telling him what? she wondered, her curiosity aroused by the girl's unexpectedly respectful manner towards him, rather as though she considered Alex to be someone important.

From what she had seen of them, Beth knew that the Czechs were a very polite and courteous nation, treating one another with courtly good manners which seemed to have gone rather out of fashion in other Western countries, but the clerk behind the desk wasn't merely treating Alex courteously; whilst her behaviour wasn't exactly obsequious, it was very definitely deferential.

Frowning a little over this perplexing insight into someone else's opinion of Alex, Beth quickly warned herself against encouraging herself to see hitherto unnoticed good points about him. She had made *that* mistake with Julian Cox, determinedly supporting him and even defending him to her closest friends when they had tried gently to warn her what kind of man he was.

She had even ignored the fact that her own best friend, Kelly, had had to reject his advances at the same time that she was actually seeing him, letting Julian persuade her that Kelly was just jealous.

Beth could hardly bear now to reflect on her own wilful foolishness. She knew that Kelly and her friends, most especially those closest to her—Anna and Dee—all believed that Julian's perfidy had broken her heart. And it was true that she had believed that he loved her, that she had allowed herself to be carried away by the fantasy he had created around them both, the romantic deception he had woven. She was, as Beth was the first to admit, someone who was inclined to be a little over-idealistic, to believe that all her geese were potential swans, so to speak.

However, even whilst Julian had been pressuring her to make plans for an elaborate engagement party, even whilst he had been swearing undying love to her, a tiny part of her had been just that little bit concerned, just that little bit wary that he was rushing things too much, that she wasn't being given time to assimilate her own feelings properly.

All her life there had been fond, loving people there to make her most important decisions for her, to relieve her of the burden of having to do so for herself. Her parents, her grandparents, even her friends, all of them loving and caring, all of them protective, all of them acting from the best possible motives. But Beth could see now that their love and their protection had taken from her the right to make her own decisions *and* her own mistakes. It wasn't their fault. It was her own. She ought to have been more assertive, less passive, less eager to be the beloved, adored child and more eager to be the respected woman. Well, all that was behind her now. For practical reasons she needed the services of an interpreter and a guide, but that was all. There was no way she needed anyone else's support or anyone else's advice in deciding what she wanted to buy for her shop.

Alex was still speaking with the girl behind the reception desk. Beth came to a quick decision. Whilst he was busy she had the perfect opportunity to get away from him. Quickly she headed towards the lift, only realising how anxious she had been that he would come after her once she was safely inside it and it was moving.

She had the lift to herself. Briefly she closed her eyes, her face burning as, without meaning to, she suddenly found herself remembering what Alex had said to her about being in a lift with her the previous day.

Angry with herself for the wayward and highly personal nature of her thoughts, she told herself determinedly that she had far better and more important things to think about than Alex Andrews.

Once inside her room, she rang down to the reception desk and informed them that she didn't want to be disturbed—under any circumstances or by anyone.

She doubted that Alex would genuinely be concerned at not being able to make contact with her. After all, she wasn't his only woman 'client', was she?

Beth frowned as she tried to analyse the feelings tensing her body when she recalled the very elegant, if undeniably older woman she had seen him with the previous evening—the evening he had told her he intended to spend with his family. She hadn't looked the sort of person who would be taken in by the attentions of a flirtatious interpreter, but then perhaps, like her, she'd recognised Alex for exactly what he was and had decided to... There had certainly been a good deal of intimacy in the closeness of their bodies as they had stood together.

Beth wrapped her arms protectively around her own body. The distasteful suspicions flooding her mind should surely have the effect of totally destroying the physical desire she had begun to feel for Alex, not feeding the unexpected jealousy she could actually feel.

Annoyed with herself, she paced the floor of her room. It was too early for her to go back to the

Square, where she had seen the gypsy, and she felt too restless to remain here in her room—as well as much too aware of the growing danger of wanting to remain alone with her own seriously undermining, intimate thoughts.

Perhaps a guided tour of the city would help to pass some of the time. Besides which, she genuinely wanted to see more of the place which had such a wonderful reputation.

Three hours later, at the end of her chosen tour, Beth had to acknowledge that she hadn't realised the breadth of Prague's varied history. She had been shown the Jewish Cemetery, and had marvelled at its antiquity. She had stood on the hillside and looked down at Prague's pretty rooftops, admiring their copper cupolas and the soft warm reds of its tiles and bricks. She had seen the castle, with its many courtyards, and wandered with the other eager members of her group along the narrow streets lined with tiny, fascinating gift shops.

Having thanked her guide for her stimulating talk, Beth excused herself, slowly making her way back towards Wenceslas Square, stopping at one point to order a sandwich and a pot of coffee at a small attractive café where she could sit outside and watch the world go by.

If anything the Square was even more crowded this evening than it had been the evening before when she had first visited it, Beth decided as she made her way through the groups of other sightseers thronging the large cobbled area. The armour-making stall, the fire-eater and the acrobats were all there, and familiar to her, barely meriting more than a second interested look as she hurried to the stall where she had met the gypsy. Not only was the Square more crowded with tourists, there also seemed to be more stalls as well, Beth recognised, and at first she thought that her stall wasn't there.

Anxiously she searched for it, her attention momentarily caught by the pathetic sight of two young children huddled in a doorway clutching a grey-faced, ominously quiet baby. She had heard that sometimes the gypsy mothers, in order to pursue their begging more easily, sedated their children by whatever means they could, including the use of drink and—appallingly, to Beth's mind—drugs.

Poor child, and poor mother too, Beth's tender heart couldn't help feeling. Whatever the rights and wrongs of their political situation—and Beth was the first to admit that she was in no position to be any judge of that—she couldn't help but feel sad for the plight of her fellow humans.

Even though she knew she was probably doing the wrong thing, she couldn't stop herself from giving the grubby child who approached her a handful of small change.

As she firmly shooed the children away, shaking her head to show that there was no more money, she saw the stall she had been looking for tucked away to one side of a larger one. Relieved, she hurried towards it.

The woman she had seen the previous evening recognised her immediately, beckoning her over with a wide smile.

'I have here the glass for you to see,' she told Beth in a conspiratorial whisper, drawing her into the canvas-covered rear of her stall.

Its canvas covering obscured the light and smelt strongly, causing Beth's throat to close up uncomfortably. There was a heavy odor in the air that might have been incense, or perhaps something a little less innocuous. Beth really didn't want to know.

'See…here it is…' the woman was telling Beth, touching her on the arm as she directed her attention to several pieces of glass she had placed on a makeshift table formed from an old box. Beth had to kneel down to see the glass properly, but once she did so she caught her breath in awed delight, instinctively reaching out to take hold of the beautifully crafted items the woman was showing her.

Only now, in the relief of having her judgement vindicated, was she able to admit to herself how very, very important it was to her to be able to tell Alex Andrews that she had managed to find her glassware without his help.

'Oh, but these are wonderful, *perfect*,' she told the woman huskily.

As she inspected them and held them, examining them carefully and holding them up to the light, despite the gypsy woman's fierce protest and the way she shielded them from the sight of anyone else by standing in front of them, Beth found it hard to believe that they were not actually genuine antiques.

But of course they couldn't possibly be. Glassware such as this, *had* it been antique, would have been locked away in a museum somewhere. To have owned glass like this in the seventeenth century one would have had to have been a very wealthy person indeed. It was, no doubt, something in the traditional manufacturing process that gave the gloss an 'antique' look.

The more she studied the pieces the gypsy woman was showing her, the more Beth's excitement grew. To be able to display glassware such as this in her shop would indeed be a wonderful coup. So far as she knew, no one had ever seen anything like it, other than in private collections or locked away behind glass doors in a handful of very expensive and up-market specialist stores. The gilding alone...

In all, the gypsy woman had brought half a dozen pieces for Beth to examine, in three slightly different styles of stemware, in cranberry, the deepest, richest blue Beth had ever seen, gold and emerald. There was a very ornate pedestal bowl, with an intricately faceted stem that caught the light as brilliantly as a flawless diamond, a breathtakingly beautiful water jug, with flowers cut into its handle and lavishly embellished with gilt, two wine glasses and, last of all, a pair of lustres even more beautiful than the ones Beth had seen in the gift shop. She wanted it all, knew she could *sell* it all if, and it was a very big if, the price was right.

There were, here and there in Europe, she knew, small factories with dedicated craftsmen that still made such articles, but at a cost that put them way, way out of the means of most people. A wealthy oil sheikh, a millionaire pop star, royal houses—*they* might be able to afford whole suites of such stemware, but her customers, even the most comfortably off of them, could not.

All Beth's original plans to purchase good-quality but relatively inexpensive plain glass crystal stemware, perhaps embellished with a discreet amount of gold, flew out of her head—and her heart—as she studied the pieces the gypsy woman displayed to her.

Her budget was relatively small, and she had no doubt that these pieces would be expensive, but Beth knew she just had to have them. Already she could see them displayed in the shop. Already she could hear the delighted gasps of their customers, the flood of sales. Her excited thoughts ran on and on whilst Beth tried as sedately as she could to elicit from the gypsy what exactly the factory *did* manufacture.

'Do these come in suites of stemware?' she asked her, picking up one of the glasses. 'A full set, or just these wine glasses?'

'A full set could be made if that was what you wanted,' the gypsy told Beth, her eyes narrowing as she added shrewdly, 'Of course, that would mean you would have to give the factory a substantial order.'

Beth's heart sank. How much exactly was a substantial order? When the gypsy told her her heart sank even further. One hundred suites of glassware in the same pattern was far more than she could ever hope to sell, unless...

'If I have so many could I have a mix of colours? Say twenty-five suites of each of the four colourways?' she asked.

The gypsy pursed her lips.

'I am not sure. I would have to check with the factory first about that.'

'And the cost?' Beth asked her quickly. 'How much is the glass? Do you have a price list?' she added.

The gypsy shook her head, her smile revealing the gap in her teeth.

'How much can you afford?' she challenged Beth.

Beth paused. Haggling had never been one of her

strong points—that was far more Kelly's forte than hers—but, driven by her desire to order the glass-ware, she named a figure per suite of glassware that allowed her some margin to bargain with.

The gypsy laughed.

'So little, and for such glass.' She shook her head. 'No,' she denied, and then she named a figure that made Beth blanch a little as she quickly worked out the cost of a total order at such figures.

'No, that is far too much,' she told the gypsy firmly, and then added, 'Perhaps I could visit the factory and speak with the manager there...'

The gypsy's eyes narrowed. Beth had the most un-comfortable impression that something she had said had amused her.

'The factory...it is very far away, a whole day...'

'A whole day.' Beth frowned.

'You can say everything you have to say to me,' the gypsy started to assure her, but Beth shook her head.

She suspected that the woman, in giving her the price, was allowing a very generous margin for her-self. Common sense told Beth that had the glass been as expensive as she was quoting then it would have been sold via one of the expensive outlets she had seen on the city's main shopping streets.

As though she had guessed what she was thinking, the gypsy suddenly pulled hard on Beth's sleeve and leaned closer to her, whispering, 'The factory, it is not owned by the Czechs. It belongs to...others... You can visit it if you wish, but...' She gave a small shrug.

'I *do* wish,' Beth told her firmly.

'Very well, then I will arrange it for you. But first

you have to make a show of good faith,' the woman told her.

Make a show of good faith? For a moment Beth was nonplussed, and then she realised that the woman was asking her for money. All she had on her was a small amount of currency, and parting with it under such circumstances went against everything she personally believed in, but she had, nevertheless, to do so.

With one last lingering inspection of the glassware, Beth made arrangements to meet with the gypsy again.

'Why not tomorrow?' she asked her, knowing that she was going to have to extend the length of her original visit if she did as the other woman wished.

'No. No, that is not possible. Arrangements have to be made,' the woman told Beth.

'Very well, then…' Beth wondered if she should offer to provide her own transport for the journey, but she was loath to involve Alex in what she was doing. After all, he was not going to be very pleased to discover that she was giving her business to someone else when he plainly wanted her to give it to his cousins.

However, before she could say anything, the gypsy was telling her, 'I will meet you here a week from now at seven o'clock in the morning. We will drive all day. You will see the factory and then we will drive back. You will bring with you some money…'

Some money. Beth looked at her in alarm.

It had been her intention to pay for any goods she ordered via her bank, but, rather than discuss this with the gypsy, she decided that she would leave the financial side of things until after she had reached the factory. She wasn't one hundred per cent sure she totally trusted the gypsy, and the truth was that if the glass she had shown her hadn't been so spectacularly beautiful and so very covetable Beth suspected she would not have entertained the idea of doing business via her.

In fact, Beth decided, as she walked back towards the hotel a little later, Prague was having the most decidedly odd effect—not just on her behaviour but also on the way she viewed herself.

Lust, the kind of healthy, energetic, empowering lust that other women were so cheerfully and self-confidently able to admit to, had never been an emotion Beth had expected herself to feel. She had always thought that emotionally she simply wasn't robust and self-motivated enough, that she simply didn't possess the energy or the confidence to say 'I want' about anything or anyone, and yet here she was, after less than a week here in Prague, being forced to admit to herself that not only did she want, but she wanted very powerfully and lustfully indeed. And she didn't just mean the beautiful glass.

Such knowledge was enough to stop her momentarily in mid-stride. Cautiously she dared to examine this admission a little more closely. Was her yearning to touch and explore the male beauty of Alex's body as powerful and compelling as the urge she had experienced to hold and caress the beautiful glass?

The heat that flooded her body gave her its own answer. In her hands the glass had felt cool and smooth, heavy and solidly curved, the raised rim of gilding sensuously rough against her fingertips in contrast to the smooth contours of the glass itself.

Would Alex's body feel the same? Heat exploded

inside her, showering her, turning her veins heavy with liquid excitement. The sensuality of her own thoughts, so completely contradictory to anything she had experienced before, totally bemused Beth, teasing and tormenting her, enticing her to explore them further.

It was growing dark. She ought to get back to the hotel, she warned herself shakily.

As she walked past the reception desk the young man on duty called her name.

'Mr Andrews has been asking for you,' he told Beth as she approached the desk. 'He has left you a message.'

Reluctantly Beth took the sealed note he was handing her, but she didn't open it until she was in her room.

I had hoped to invite you to join my cousins and myself for dinner this evening, but unfortunately I could not make contact with you. I shall pick you up at the hotel in the morning at ten o'clock unless I hear from you to the contrary. If you wish to telephone me the number is…

Just for a moment Beth was tempted to dial the number and tell him triumphantly that she had found the glass she wanted, and without his help, but common sense warned her that this would not be a good idea. Especially since it seemed obvious that he had still not given up hope of persuading her to buy from his family, if his statement about intending to ask her to have dinner with them was anything to go by.

Had he taken someone else to meet them instead…that elegant older woman, perhaps? Deter-

minedly Beth pushed him out of her thoughts. There
were things she had to do. She was still bubbling
over with excitement about what she had seen and
longing to share the excitement with someone. It was
too late now to ring Kelly, but she would do so tomorrow. She would have to ring her bank as well,
but that could wait until after she had visited the
factory. Beth wasn't sure how she was going to be
able to wait.

Squeezing her eyes tightly closed, she tried to vi-
sualise the glass she had seen, but, infuriatingly, the
image that formed behind her closed eyelids wasn't
that of the beautiful glassware but of Alex Andrews'
strong, masculine features, his compellingly unusual
steel-grey eyes smouldering with a mercurial heat
that made her heart flip excitedly against her chest
wall and her stomach muscles contract with sensual
urgency.

CHAPTER SIX

BETH woke up, her body tensing as she recognised from the strength of the light filtering through her hotel bedroom curtains that she had slept beyond her normal waking-up time.

And then she started to relax as she remembered that this morning she did not have to get up early, since today she was not planning to visit any factories.

The decision she had made late last night to leave a message for Alex Andrews on his answer-machine, thanking him for his help but stating quite firmly that she now no longer needed his services and asking him to leave her a bill, had, rather oddly, not given her quite as much satisfaction as she had anticipated.

Beth frowned as she climbed out of bed and walked naked into her bathroom.

The weight she had lost in the trauma following the break-up of her relationship with Julian had now been replaced, banishing the hollow-eyed gauntness which had not suited her small curvy frame.

Prague had brought the sheen back to her hair and the glow back to her skin.

Quickly she showered and put on clean undies, then blow-dried her hair. She had just finished high-lighting her naturally delicate and pale skin with blusher and applying her lipstick when she heard the room service waiter knocking.

Quickly she reached for her robe and, wrapping it tightly around her body, she went to let him in.

'Thank you, that's...' she began, and then stopped as she realised that the man pushing the trolley wasn't her normal room service waiter but Alex Andrews. Her eyes widened even further as she saw that the table wasn't set up just for one but for two.

'What are *you* doing here?' she demanded in angry confusion, instinctively pulling the robe even more tightly around her body. But as Alex set up the table Beth was treacherously aware of how glad she was that he hadn't arrived before she had had time to wash her hair and do her face; after all, why should she mind whether or not Alex saw her at her best or her worst?

She was simply reacting in a totally normal female way, she defended herself mentally. There was nothing personal in her reaction; she would have felt the same no matter who had arrived with the tray.

Would she?

Beth fought to suppress the knowledge that only yesterday, when the room service waiter had arrived, it hadn't concerned her in the least that she had had to let him in with her hair uncombed and her face still pale from sleep.

'I thought we could discuss what we are going to do today over breakfast,' Alex replied cheerfully as he pulled up a chair for her with a very professional flourish and waved her into it.

Too caught off guard to refuse, Beth automatically sat down.

'*We* are not going to do anything,' she informed him firmly. 'Didn't you get my message?'

'You don't intend to visit any more factories. Yes,

I know,' Alex agreed. 'However, there is far, far more to Prague and the Republic than glass factories.'

'I'm sure there is, and I'm looking forward to discovering it and them—on my own,' Beth told him pointedly.

'I thought we'd start with a walk round the city,' Alex continued, expertly pouring Beth's coffee and then sitting down opposite her and offering her a piece of toast.

'You have no right to do this, nor to be here,' Beth told him furiously. 'I could report you to the hotel manager…'

She could, but Beth knew that she wouldn't. Someone, whether her official waiter or someone else, must have known what Alex was doing, and to report them might be to get them into trouble. Beth was far too soft-hearted·to do that, and she suspected that Alex knew it.

'Why don't you want to visit any more factories?' Alex was asking her, ignoring her patently weak threat.

'Because I don't need to,' Beth told him promptly, adding, 'Not that it's any of your business…' But instead of looking suitably chastised Alex was actually looking quite stern.

'Beth, you aren't still thinking of following up that contact you made in the Square, are you? Because if you are…'

'*If* I am, then it's *my* business and no one else's,' Beth told him furiously. How dared he try to tell her what she could and could not do, and, even worse, how dared he try to make her feel as though she was a gullible little fool, incapable of making a rational or informed business decision?

'And despite what *you* seem to think I actually do know my own business and my own customers,' she continued hotly. 'I know what will and won't sell in *my* shop, and at what price, and if *you* think—'

'I'm sorry. I'm sorry,' Alex apologised remorsefully. 'I wasn't trying to imply that you don't know your own business, Beth, or your own market, but buying goods here in the Republic isn't quite like going on a buying trip at home. The Czech people themselves couldn't be more honest, but there are other forces at work here, other…problems…which have to be taken into account.

'If you really feel that this gypsy contact you've made *is* genuine, then at least allow me to come with you when you go to visit the factory…'

'Why? So that you can get the opportunity to undercut their prices and point me in the direction of your cousins' factory instead?' Beth demanded sharply, adding scornfully, 'You see, Alex, I'm not *quite* so naive as you seem to think. I'm perfectly well aware of what you're trying to do. No doubt the reason you're here today is really to try to persuade me to visit your precious cousins' business…'

Beth saw from the look on his face that her guess was right, but instead of feeling triumphant she discovered that the tiny needle-sharp sensation knowing she was right gave her actually physically hurt.

'I *had* intended to suggest that it might be worthwhile your visiting the factory, yes,' Alex agreed, his voice suddenly unfamiliarly harsh. 'But not for the less than altruistic reasons you're trying to suggest.

If you must have the truth, the glass my cousins—'
He stopped.

'What *is* it about you, Beth? Why is it you're so
determined to suspect my motives?'

Beth pushed away her toast uneaten.

'You're a man,' she told him acidly, 'and my experience of men is that…'

There was a small, tight silence, and then Alex
said harshly, 'Do go on. Your experience of men is
what?'

Beth looked away from him. Something about the
tight white line around his mouth was hurting her.
Without knowing how it had happened she had
strayed onto some very treacherous and uncertain
ground indeed. What on earth had possessed her to
raise a subject both so intimately personal and so
volatilely dangerous?

'So, I'm to be condemned without a hearing, is
that it? Sentenced for a crime I haven't even committed simply because I'm a man… Who was he,
Beth?' he asked her grimly. 'A friend? A lover?'

Beth discovered that she was finding it hard to
swallow. Completely unexpectedly and totally un-
wontedly she found that her eyes had filled with
tears.

'Actually he was neither,' she told Alex shakily,
and then, before she could stop herself, she was adding emotionally, 'If you must know he was the man
who told me he loved me but didn't—the man who
betrayed me and…'

Frantically she got up, her eyes flooding with tears,
knocking over her chair in her desperate attempt to
avoid crying in front of Alex and completely humil-
iating herself. But as she tried to run to the sanctuary

of the bathroom the length of her bathrobe hampered her, and she had only taken a few steps before Alex caught up with her, bodily grabbed hold of her and swung her round to face him, his own face taut with emotion.

'Oh, Beth. Beth, please don't cry,' she heard him groan as he wrapped her in his arms. 'I'm so sorry…I didn't mean to upset you. I never…'

'I'm not upset,' Beth denied. 'I didn't love him anyway,' she told Alex truthfully, and then added less honestly, 'Men aren't worth loving…'

'No?' Alex asked her huskily.

'No,' Beth repeated firmly, but somehow or other her denial had lost a good deal of its potency. Was that perhaps because of the way Alex was cupping her face, his mouth gently caressing hers, his lips teasing the stubbornly tight line of hers, coaxing it to soften and part on a soft sigh that should have been a sharp rejection of what he was doing but somehow had become something softer and more accommodating?

As Alex continued to kiss her the most dizzying sweet sensation filled Beth.

She had the most overpowering urge to cling blissfully to Alex and melt into his arms like an old-fashioned Victorian maiden. Behind her closed eyelids she could have sworn there danced sunlit images of tulle and confetti scented with the lilies of a bridal bouquet, and the sound of a triumphant 'Wedding March' swelled and boomed and gold sunbeams formed a circle around her.

Dreamily Beth sighed, and then smiled beneath Alex's kiss, her own lips parting in happy acquiescence to the explorative thrust of his tongue.

Alex was dressed casually, in jeans and a soft shirt. Beneath her fingertips Beth could feel the fabric of that shirt, soft and warm, but the body that lay beneath it felt deliciously firm...hard, masculine, an unfamiliar and even forbidden territory that her fingers were suddenly dangerously eager to explore.

Alex made a small sound of approving pleasure as Beth's fingers rebelliously slipped between the buttons of his shirt. Her borrowed hotel robe, a 'one size fits all' garment of extremely generous proportions, was starting to slide off her shoulder, and the sensation of Alex's fingertips just brushing her bare skin sent a violent frisson of breathtaking pleasure zigzagging all down her body.

Beth wasn't used to such an explosive physical reaction to a man's touch. It made her catch her breath, her mouth rounding and her teeth accidentally closing on the fullness of Alex's bottom lip and dragging gently against it.

Alex gave a thickly audible responsive groan that shivered through her own body right down to her toes, making her curl them into the carpet. The sensual heat they were both generating was combining to melt away all Beth's inhibitions, her mouth opening eagerly to the demanding thrust of Alex's tongue.

Her robe had started to open when she had trodden on the hem during her earlier attempt to escape from the humiliation of her own tears, but Beth was totally unaware of just how much of her body it had actually exposed until she felt the warmth of Alex's hand against her breast, firmly cupping its soft weight against his palm as he slowly caressed its rounded shape with a slow, sensuous deliberation that made Beth tremble and then shudder, the rash of goosebumps raised on her skin betraying just how immediately and intensely sensitive she was to the erotic sensation of his caress.

Over Alex's shoulder she could see their entwined images in her bedroom mirror. His hand, tanned and brown, lean and muscular, in direct contrast to the pale, sheer fabric-covered globe of her breast, soft, full, rounded, compliant to his touch. Male to female, man to woman, hard against soft.

Alex was still kissing her, plundering her mouth, his free hand burrowing beneath her robe to rest just below her waist on her naked back, his fingers stroking, kneading her sensitive flesh into such a frenzy of responsiveness that she was pressing herself frantically against him, mindlessly grinding her hips into his body, desperately searching for even closer contact with his aroused hardness.

The hand caressing her breast started to stroke it rhythmically, Alex's fingertips teasing her nipple to a stiff point beneath her gauzy bra, playing with it, flicking it with a tormenting gentleness that made Beth tremble from head to foot with hungry need.

In the mirror now their bodies were so closely entwined, so *sensuously* entwined, that they might almost already have been lovers. Beth moaned longingly, reaching out to cover Alex's hand with her own, wanting to urge him to remove the barrier of her bra. She was acting on instinct alone now, driven by a female urge programmed into her by nature itself, and, in obeying it, she had as little choice as a lemming following its preordained life path.

When Alex resisted her attempt to guide him to do what she wanted she growled her female frustration at having her need left unsatisfied beneath his kiss, making a low, keening sound that had no words but which Alex seemed immediately able to translate.

'I can't,' he told her hoarsely, his hand burning hot against her swollen breast. 'If I do, if I see you…touch you…'

His eyes flashed signals of stormy male desire, the sweetly savage bite of his teeth against the tenderness of her kiss-sensitive lips betraying how he would treat the tormenting and tormented sensitivity of her aroused nipples if she made him remove their frail protective covering. But Beth had gone beyond the safety of heeding any kind of warning.

Something—she neither knew nor cared what—had snapped the taut barrier she had wrapped around her feelings, her responses, her right to enjoy her female sexuality.

It was as though all the hurt she had experienced, all the anger, all the fear and distress, the humiliation and the pain had coalesced, exploded, burned itself out in a fierce transmuting heat that had turned her from her previously shy, inhibited, immature self into a powerfully strong and sexually motivated woman, a woman whose body demanded, expected and *intended* to have nothing less than total satisfaction of its deepest and most privately, primitively intimate sexual desires.

To her own shock, and her own fierce joy, she recognised that the Beth who had imagined the only way she could ever really enjoy sex would be in the arms of a gentle, considerate lover who would treat her as carefully as a delicately made piece of fragile glass had suddenly been replaced by a Beth who knew instinctively that what she wanted now was to enjoy sex in its rawest, purest, hottest form possible.

Like the silica at its most molten fluid form, she wanted to be taken into the creative care of an expert, an artist, a master of his craft—and of her. She wanted to watch, to be, as he poured the golden liquid form of her being into the crucible of heat that was their mutual desire. She wanted to feel the sharply passionate grate of his teeth against her tender flesh, to feel him being driven by his desire for her in the same way that Adam had been driven to eat the forbidden fruit handed to him by Eve. *She* wanted to be Alex's forbidden fruit, she recognised dazedly.

'Do it,' she commanded him tautly, dragging his hand down so that his fingers caught in the edge of her bra, revealing the soft shimmer of her naked skin and the beginnings of the wantonly dark areola of her nipple.

Her robe was fully open now, and hanging off her arms. In the mirror Beth could see her own near-naked body.

'Do it,' she repeated hypnotically, her eyes wide and dark as she stared up into Alex's.

'You don't know what...' he began, but Beth shook her head.

'Do it,' she told him a third time, holding his gaze as she let her own hand drop away from his.

She could feel his fingers trembling oh, so slightly as he splayed them across her breast, almost as though he wanted to cover her, protect her modesty, and then they tensed and curled and his thumb-tip rubbed across her tightly erect nipple, once, twice, a third time, each time lingering just a breath of time longer against the erect peak.

And then, agonisingly slowly, he very carefully

peeled the fine fabric away from her breast completely.

Deep down in her throat Beth made a long, keening sound of female yearning.

In the mirror she could see the robe trailing on the floor behind her as Alex slowly released her and then very unsteadily took a step back from her.

Blindly Beth followed him.

Her body ached with need and heat, and yet the distance that Alex had put between them made her shiver with cold and loss. Instinctively she sought the warmth of his body against her, instinctively she tried to recapture it, moving closer to him, a small half-cry of protest locking her throat as her feet became caught up in the heavy folds of her robe.

As Alex reached out to help her she straightened her arms impatiently, thrusting at the cumbersome folds of the robe. Alex dropped to his knees in front of her, almost as though he intended to stop her or restrain her, but it was already too late. Already the robe had fallen back from her body.

Because her room wasn't overlooked Beth didn't fully close the drapes at night, and now the bright sunshine flooding through the gauzy nets revealed her body in all its exquisitely feminine detail. She could see herself in the mirror, and she could see Alex as well.

The hands he had put out to hold her dropped to her waist, shaping its narrow slenderness, his concentration on his exploration of her so intense that Beth scarcely dared to breathe in case she broke it.

His hands moved lower, cradling her hips. Alex leaned forward and very gently kissed her softly rounded belly, the caress of his lips the merest whisper of pleasure and promise but still more than enough to create a reaction that shuddered right through Beth's body.

Alex's head was moving upwards, his tongue-tip trailing hot darts of fire over her waist and then her ribcage. Alex's hands left her hips and his fingers encircled her towelling-clad wrists, then moved upwards to grip the sleeves of her robe as though he intended to pull it back onto her body. Instinctively Beth stiffened in rejection of what she thought he was going to do, resisting his rejection—of her. Alex lifted his head and looked into her eyes. Turbulently Beth looked back at him, a ragged breath tearing at her lungs.

She heard Alex groan, and then shockingly, excitingly, he was wrenching the robe completely free of her body and wrapping his arms possessively around her, his fingers trembling as he tugged at the fastening of her bra, his lips, his mouth, fastening eagerly over the crest of one of her breasts and tugging sensuously on it.

Beth felt faint with liquid, dizzyingly dazzling, wanton pleasure. Her hands reached out to clasp Alex's head and hold him against her body, her fingers sliding into the thick richness of his hair, tugging at it, kneading his scalp, small purring noises escaping from her throat as she moved as sensuously against him as a cat being stroked, every movement of her body against his sinuous and hypnotic.

Through half-closed eyes she saw their combined images in the mirror, images that once would have shocked and distressed her but which now merely added even greater fuel to the fire that burned through her. The sight of Alex's head against her breast, the creaminess of her skin against the darkness of his hair, the dark rigidity of her nipple demanding that it be given parity with its twin, the colour that burned Alex's face, the moist sheen she could see on her breast as he transferred his attentions from one nipple to the other—all of them combined to add to the intensity of the visual image of her own sensuality.

There was something so pagan about the whole image, about her virtual nakedness, only the sheer flimsiness of her very brief briefs a teasing barrier to Alex's hands and touch, her head thrown back in pure sensual enjoyment, her breasts full and passion-tipped, and Alex on his knees in front of her, at once both her supplicant and her master, her feminine power momentarily controlling his much stronger masculine strength. Her desire controlling his, controlling him.

She was the raw material of the beauty they could create together; he was the one who would mould it, shape it, the one who would mould and shape her. Her feelings, her thoughts, her emotions were so elemental, so intense, so powerful that Beth was held totally in thrall to them.

For the first time in her life she was tasting the full power of her womanhood, and she—

Abruptly she tensed as she heard someone rattling her bedroom door warningly.

Immediately she froze, looking wildly for her robe, but Alex was already on his feet, wrapping it round her, allowing her to flee to the sanctuary of her bathroom.

*   *   *

'Beth…it's all right, he's gone…you can come out now.'

Beth gnawed at her bottom lip.

In the five minutes or so it had taken the waiter to clear away their uneaten breakfast she had come back down to earth with a savage, spine-jarring, emotion-lurching and generally guilt-racked thud.

What on earth had she been doing—and why? All right, so sexually she was attracted to Alex, but that didn't mean that she had to act like a hormone-driven teenager, for heaven's sake. A hormone-driven teen-ager or a frustrated, sexually unsatisfied twenty-four-year-old woman.

Beth wasn't sure which image of herself she liked the least. Which image… Her face burned as she caught sight of herself in the bathroom mirror and her thoughts strayed betrayingly to those other im-ages she had recently seen of herself.

'Beth,' Alex was repeating. 'It's okay, he's gone…'

She would have to go out sooner or later. She couldn't stay here all day, and anyway, why should she be the one to feel conscience-stricken and un-comfortable? she asked herself sturdily. After all, Alex had been just as carried away as she had herself, just as driven by desire and lust… But to be driven by lust was perfectly acceptable for a man, whereas…

These days it was just as acceptable for a woman, Beth told herself firmly. These days a woman no longer had to be fettered by the old shibboleths that had denied them their own sexuality and the right to express it. These days a woman did not have to con-vince herself that she loved a man just in order to enjoy her physical desire for his body and her own satisfaction. No, indeed… So why was she cowering here in the bathroom as though…as though she had done something to feel ashamed of? She *wasn't*…she *hadn't*…she told herself fiercely as she tugged open the bathroom door.

Determinedly she gave a businesslike glance at her watch as she told Alex crisply, with only just a hint of a tremor in her voice, 'I really think you ought to leave. I've got rather a lot I want to do today…'

Alex was frowning at her.

'I thought you said you were having a day off and that you wanted to do some sightseeing…'

Beth frowned in vexation.

'Yes. Yes, I did…I do… But…'

'It's raining now—the city should be relatively free of tourists. I suggest we start with a walk along the river. We could have lunch here in Prague, and then this afternoon…'

He stopped and gave her a look of heart-stopping intimacy. 'This afternoon we shall walk over the Charles Bridge…and then there's something special I want to show you…'

Beth opened her mouth to tell him that he was taking far too much for granted, that she didn't want his company, that she didn't want anything from him, but instead, and much to her own chagrin, she heard herself telling him, 'I…I need to get dressed. I…'

'You want me to leave.' Alex gave her a deliciously intimate smile. 'I know what you're saying,' he agreed huskily. 'If I stay here with you there's no way I'm going to be able… Tempted though I am, this is neither the time nor the place. Tempted though I am,' he repeated. He closed the distance between them and murmured against her lips, 'And believe me, Bethany, I am very, very tempted. Oh, yes, I am very tempted...'

Beth told herself that she was trying to resist him, and that the only reason she'd opened her mouth was to tell him to stop, but unfortunately he seemed to mistake her actions, and the next thing she knew he was kissing her with a renewal of the passion he had shown earlier. But this time he didn't take it any further. This time he released her and stepped back from her, gently pressing his fingers to his own mouth and then touching them lightly to hers before telling her huskily, 'I'll come back for you in half an hour.'

CHAPTER SEVEN

BETH flicked the droplets of rain off her jacket and stared across the mist-shrouded vista in front of her. She and Alex were looking along the river, its bridges, so clearly depicted in so many tourist postcards, now barely discernible. The artists who normally thronged the streets selling their work to the tourists had already packed away their sketches, only an enterprising umbrella seller standing his ground.

'My, I never expected it to rain, not after how bright it was this morning!' Beth heard an American voice exclaim. She still had no real idea just why she had allowed Alex to persuade her to come with him. It had certainly not been her intention when she'd woken up this morning. A pink glow of self-consciousness coloured her face as her senses told her exactly why she might have changed her mind. Of course, her decision had nothing to do with that most unfortunate incident in her bedroom earlier this morning. Nothing whatsoever. That had been a mistake…a…a…

'Look,' Alex told her, taking hold of her arm and directing her attention to the hillside to their left. As he did so Alex drew Beth closer to him. It was just because the heavy drenching rain was making her feel damp and chilly that she felt this desire to nestle closer to him, Beth assured herself. That was all… It was simply a basic human need for warmth that was causing her to accept the warmth of his protective arm and the even greater warmth of his body.

They had lunch in a small traditional restaurant where the patron obviously knew Alex and welcomed him enthusiastically. But to Beth's consternation the man seemed to be under the misapprehension that Beth was Alex's girlfriend.

'There will be a big wedding here in Prague… yes?' he said jovially to Alex. 'We have many fine churches here,' he told Beth.

'Why did you let him think that?' Beth asked Alex later, when they had left the restaurant.

'Why did I let him think what?' Alex teased her, pretending not to understand.

Beth flashed him an indignant look.

'You know what I mean,' she accused him. '*Why* did you let him think that we are…?'

'What? A couple…lovers…? Is it so very far from the truth?' Alex asked her meaningfully.

'We hardly know one another,' Beth protested. Why was he doing this…pretending to genuinely care about her? She could understand him trying to flirt with her in order to secure her business, both for himself and for his family, but to try to pretend that there was more to what he was doing than mere flirtation…

'I want to go back to the hotel,' she told him curtly. 'There are things I have to do…'

'Not yet,' Alex denied, taking hold of her arm before she could stop him and drawing her in the direction of the river.

Up ahead of them Beth could see the ancient span of the Charles Bridge.

Awed by its antiquity, and her own awareness of

all that it must have witnessed and withstood, Beth allowed him to guide her towards it. There was something about it, a stalwartness, a sombreness, that struck an unexpected chord within her.

'My grandfather once told me that always, in his darkest moments, he thought of this bridge and all that it and his people had endured,' Alex told her quietly.

His quiet, soft-voiced comment, so very much in tune with her own unspoken thoughts, shocked her a little. They weren't supposed to be so emotionally in accord; they shouldn't be able to pick up on each other's thoughts.

In an attempt to distance herself from what she was feeling, Beth said quickly, 'Tell me more about your grandfather.'

Alex was smiling at her. A smile that rocked her heart. Fiercely she reminded herself of all the reasons why she could not allow herself to respond to him.

Whilst Alex was talking to her about his grandfather the rain started to come down even more heavily.

'Quick, down here,' he broke off to instruct her, taking hold of her hand and hurrying her towards a small alcove set protectively into the last span of the bridge.

Without thinking, Beth automatically followed him. In the shelter it provided them with she could see Alex looking searchingly at her. Her heart started to beat far too fast.

'Beth, I know it's probably too soon to tell you this, but I think I'm falling in…' He stopped and looked down into her eyes. 'It's crazy, I know, but I've fallen in love with you,' he groaned.

'*No!*' Immediately Beth panicked. 'No, that's not possible,' she denied. 'I don't want to hear this, Alex…'

Inside she felt as though she was being torn apart. Did he really think she was foolish enough, desperate enough, vulnerable enough to fall for his lies?

Beth was slightly more familiar with the city now, and she knew from the direction they were taking that they were walking back to the hotel. It was still raining—heavily—but even though she told herself that it would be a relief to be free of Alex there was still an uncomfortable heaviness around her heart.

The after-effects of her lunch and the distinctive and disturbing ache she was still suffering after this morning's interrupted lovemaking, Beth assured herself stoically. That was all. There was no emotional base to what she was feeling. How could there be? She felt nothing emotional for Alex at all… If she had wanted him…needed him…been *aroused* by him, then that had simply been a sexual wanting, a sexual needing, a sexual arousal. There had been nothing emotional about it. Nothing… Men didn't have the power to affect her emotionally any more. She didn't like them…didn't trust them… She was far better off on her own, using them in the way that they used her sex.

They had reached the hotel. Beth was just about to hurry towards the main entrance when Alex caught hold of her wrist.

'No, this way,' he instructed her, moving off in the direction of the car park and tugging her with him.

'Where are we going? Where are you taking me?'

Beth asked as Alex unlocked the door of his hire car, refusing to release her until he had carefully tucked her into the passenger seat.

'Wait and see. It's a surprise,' he told her teasingly as he slid into the driver's seat next to her and started the engine.

A surprise.

Beth looked suspiciously at him.

'This isn't just a ploy to get me to visit your cousins' business, is it?' she accused him. 'Because if it is...'

She stopped as she saw that Alex was frowning at her.

'No, it isn't a ploy,' he denied. 'Although why... *what* is it that makes you so mistrustful of me, Beth? Is it this man, the one who hurt you?'

'He didn't hurt me,' Beth denied. 'I never loved him. I just... From the moment I arrived here you've done nothing but flatter me and flirt with me...'

'And that makes me someone you can't trust?' Alex asked her quietly.

Something about the way he was looking at her made Beth feel slightly ashamed.

'I don't want to talk about it, Alex. Where are we going? I don't...'

'Wait and see,' he repeated, and then added softly, 'Tell me about yourself, Beth.'

'There isn't anything to tell,' she protested shakily. 'I'm not someone who's either interesting or exciting.'

'You are to me,' Alex assured her with a soft emphasis that made the tiny hairs on her skin lift in sensual awareness.

Beth hadn't intended to do what he asked, but

somehow or other she discovered that she was, albeit a little reluctantly at first.

'Your family sounds very much like my own,' Alex interrupted her at one point. 'My mother was always very conscious of the fact that she had no family of her own in England. The Czech people are very extended-family-conscious.'

They had left the city now, and were climbing through the hills—not that Beth could see much of them because of the heavy black clouds. The rain was causing rivulets of water to run down the surface of the road, carrying with them bits of debris. In the distance she could hear thunder which, although it didn't exactly terrify her, was not something she enjoyed.

'The weather is a lot more severe than was forecast,' Alex commented frowningly at one point, when he had had to drop the car down to a low gear to drive through a deep pool of water which had collected in the dip in the road.

'Perhaps we should turn back,' Beth suggested uneasily. She still had no idea where they were going, but they were well into the hills now, and the villages they were driving through were small, little more than clusters of houses, many of them unoccupied. Alex had explained to her that most people owned houses in the villages but because they worked in the city were only able to use them for weekends and holidays.

They were climbing higher now, through a grey, mist-enshrouded landscape that made Beth shiver a little involuntarily. Where on earth was Alex taking her?

'You're looking apprehensive. There's no need,'

he reassured her, and then added wryly, 'You're safe with me, Beth, but has it occurred to you that you might not have been had you agreed to accompany your gypsy friends to wherever it was they claimed they were going to take you?'

Beth bit her lip and looked studiedly out of the car window. Alex seemed to think that she had given up her plans to go and visit the glass factory, but she hadn't…not that she intended to tell him that—or anything else about her intentions. Why should she?

'Not much further now,' he told her as he changed down a gear for the steep hill they were climbing.

Beth gasped, instinctively clinging onto her seat as they crested the mist-shrouded hill and then abruptly started to drop straight down, the road in front of them almost perpendicular, she was sure. At the bottom they had to ford what amounted to a racing stream of swirling water.

Alex grimaced when he saw her expression as she looked out of the car window.

'It's the rain,' he told her. 'This culvert makes a natural channel for it. In the old days there was actually a river here, but it was diverted.

'No questions,' he warned Beth as she started to open her mouth. 'Please close your eyes. We're almost there.'

Almost where…?

Beth was just about to object when a sudden ferocious clap of thunder made her close them instinctively. The intensity with which the rain was drumming down on the car roof suddenly seemed to treble as they started to climb again. Beth could see the jagged flashes of lightning behind her closed eyelids, but the ferocity of the storm which was raging around them made her feel too apprehensive to open her eyes.

'Where *are* we going?' Beth protested, unable to keep the betraying tremor out of her voice.

'It's a surprise,' she heard Alex repeating to her. 'Have you still got your eyes closed?'

Obediently Beth nodded, then gasped as the car rattled noisily over what sounded like a wooden bridge and started to climb a steep hillside, before levelling out, crunching over gravel and then coming to a halt.

'You can open them now,' she heard Alex saying softly in her ear, his voice sending delicious little shivers of sensation, like subtle harbingers of pleasure to come, along her sensitive nerve-endings.

Quickly Beth opened her eyes, and then widened them in stunned awe as she took in the splendour of her surroundings.

'Where on earth are we?' she whispered a little hesitantly. 'It looks like a castle...'

'That's exactly what it is,' Alex replied promptly.

Stunned, Beth stared at the creamy white walls in front of her, with their small slit windows and their dome-capped turrets. Too solidly built to be the fairy-tale castle of a little girl's fantasies, this one was built much more on the lines of an awesome stronghold. A curtain wall surrounded the courtyard they were in, and as Beth swivelled round she could see the steep incline they had climbed to reach the plateau area of the courtyard. In front of them a flight of stone steps curled away around the side of the building, and two huge arched wooden doors were ominously closed in front of them.

'What are we doing here? What…what is this place?' Beth asked.

'Want to take a closer look?' Alex invited her, opening his own car door.

Bemused, Beth nodded.

The air outside was colder than she had expected, and wetter. The rain she had heard beating down on the car roof during the drive had intensified in severity, striking her exposed face and legs so hard it almost hurt.

The mountainside the castle was built on was so high that it was actually above the mist. On a clear day the view must be awesome, Beth acknowledged. Right now she felt almost intimidated by the savagery of the lashing rain and the noise of the thunder rumbling in the distance.

'Quick…this way,' Alex told her, sheltering her in the curve of his arm as he hurried her towards the massive double doors. Once they reached them Beth saw that a small door was cut into them, which Alex unlocked with a key he produced from his jacket pocket.

Once through the door and out of the rain Beth saw that they were in a huge stone-flagged hall, with a fireplace along one wall that was almost the size of her sitting room at home. If anything the air inside the hall was even colder than outside it.

'I hadn't realised the weather was going to be quite so bad as this when I planned this trip,' Alex told her ruefully as he led the way to the back of the hall and into a narrow passage.

As she followed him up a dark flight of stone stairs Beth felt almost as though she had strayed into an *Alice in Wonderland* setting.

The stairs turned and twisted, illuminated by the light from heavy wrought-iron fittings, flickering hazardously as though threatening to go out at any second, and then suddenly they were stepping onto a large wood-floored landing area, with larger, more graceful windows and an intricate design set into the parquet of the floor.

'This is the more modern part of the castle. It was built on in 1760 by I forget which ancestor. My aunt gets quite severely cross with me for not being able to remember all the details of our family history. I suspect she thinks I don't pay attention when she's relating it to me.'

'Your aunt…your family owns *this*?' Beth gasped. He had already told her about the family's castle, of course, but she had not expected anything so grand!

'It's not so unusual—not here,' Alex told her easily. 'There are families who, after the repatriation of property following on from the Velvet Revolution, now own a handful of such places. Fortunately for us we only ever owned this one. I say fortunately because the cost of maintaining such homes can be prohibitive, as you can imagine.

'In my family's case we were fortunate in that much of the original furniture had been left *in situ*, and the castle had been lived in by a government official—or rather a succession of them—rather than simply left empty. Some of the more valuable pieces have gone, of course, and the paintings—family portraits in the main.

'As with many others of its type, the renovations to the original castle were done at the height of the influence of the Hapsburgs; there is a very strong

Viennese influence in the decor of the state apartments. Let me show you.'

Still trying to take in the fact that this place, this castle, belonged to Alex's family, Beth followed him in bemusement as he led the way through a succession of rooms that made Beth feel as though she had stepped back in time. Although she was familiar with the style and decor of many of the great houses at home, the intricately lavish rococo plasterwork which decorated the walls and ceilings of the rooms she walked through made her gasp a little in wonderment.

In one room, a salon of elegant proportions, she couldn't help staring in delight at the soft watery green of the paintwork. Mirrors alternating with pastoral scenes decorated the walls, and hanging from the centre of the ceiling was the most magnificent chandelier she had ever seen.

'Ah, yes, that was how the family originally came to own the castle in the first place,' Alex told her ruefully. 'They made chandeliers for the Hapsburg court.'

'Does your family actually live here?' Beth asked him in an awed whisper.

'When they *are* here, yes. Although the state rooms are only used on formal occasions. The whole family comes and goes pretty much at will, although during the working week my cousins and my aunt stay in Prague, where they own a large apartment. This is the drawing room the family uses,' Alex informed her, taking her through into another elegantly proportioned room which, whilst still magnificent, was less heavily decorated than the rooms she had just seen—and more comfortably furnished.

'Are any members of your family here now?' Beth asked him curiously.

Alex shook his head, frowning as he saw the way she shivered and then going over to the fire which was made up in the grate. Kneeling down to remove a box of matches from a pretty covered box, he lit the fire.

'No. My aunt would have been here, but there was a burglary at the factory recently. Some antique glass was stolen—my aunt is very distressed. She blames herself. My cousins, her sons, have been urging her for some time to have a more up-to-date burglar and security system fitted at the factory as the collection of antique glassware they have there is quite unique. They have samples of the kind of glass they make going back right to the late 1600s—but my aunt, who is very much a traditionalist and a matriarch of the old school, wanted to wait until their current night-watchman, who is approaching retirement, had actually left.

'She told my cousins that it would offend Peter's pride if they were to install a security system whilst he was still there, and she didn't want to hurt him by doing so. Now she says that because of her stubbornness not only has a priceless collection of glass been stolen, but, even worse, Peter is in hospital with concussion, having been hit on the head by the gang who broke in.'

'Oh, no!' Beth couldn't help exclaiming in distress as she listened to him. 'Will he…the night-watchman…be all right?'

'We hope so. But until she knows that he has recovered my aunt refuses to leave the city.'

'Does she know you've brought me here…to her home? Will she mind?'

Alex shook his head.

'It was her suggestion that I do so. She is immensely proud of our family tradition and of this place.'

'Yes, I'm sure she is,' Beth agreed.

The heat from the fire was beginning to warm her chilled body, but she still winced as lightning tore a jagged line right through the thick greyness of the mist outside. There was a loud clap of thunder and then almost immediately another flash of lightning.

'Don't worry, we're safe in here,' Alex comforted her, adding more prosaically, 'Are you hungry?'

Beth discovered a little to her own surprise that she was, and nodded.

'You stay here, then,' Alex instructed her. 'I shan't be long.'

He was gone about fifteen minutes, long enough for Beth to be curious enough to wander around the room studying the family photographs decorating the highly polished surfaces of the heavy wooden furniture.

In one of them an unexpectedly familiar face stared back at her. Picking it up, she studied it.

She was still holding it a few seconds later when Alex returned, carrying what looked like a large picnic hamper.

'Is this your aunt?' she asked him, holding the photograph she had been studying out to him.

'Yes. It is,' he confirmed, smiling at her. 'How did you guess?'

Beth said nothing. She wasn't going to tell him that she had known because she'd recognised the woman as the same one she had seen him with in the hotel in Prague, and then at the opera, and she certainly wasn't going to tell him just what assumptions she had made about the two of them. It had never occurred to her that the elegant and obviously expensively dressed woman might be a member of Alex's family, and not a rich tourist for whom he was working.

'Food,' Alex informed her as he put the hamper down. 'I'll just—' He broke off as the thunder crashed again and all the lights suddenly went out.

Cursing, Alex told her ruefully, 'I should have guessed this might happen. Fortunately my aunt always keeps a supply of candles to hand in every room. The electricity supply here is notorious for its unreliability, and these storms don't exactly help.' As he spoke he was pulling open the drawers in a pretty sofa table and setting candles in a couple of heavy silver candelabra on the mantelpiece above the fire.

'We'll have to picnic in here, I'm afraid,' he told Beth as he placed one on the table behind the sofa. Outside it had suddenly gone very dark, the wind driving the rain so hard at the windows that Beth could hear the fierce sound it made.

'Perhaps we ought to make our way back to Prague,' she suggested nervously, remembering how hazardous their journey to the castle had been.

But Alex seemed to misunderstand the cause of her apprehension, coming to stand close to her as he asked her softly, 'What is it you're afraid of, Beth? Not me?'

'No, of course not,' she denied, and then, for some reason she couldn't understand herself, she discovered that she couldn't quite bring herself to look at him, and the feeling that was curling up right through her body had far more to do with a dangerous sense of forbidden excitement than with any kind of fear.

There was something undeniably erotic about being here alone with him in this timeless place, and the lack of the modern amenity of electric light, the softness of the fire and candlelight, only served to highlight the sensation that filled her that she might have been transported back in time, to a time when for a young woman to be alone with a young man had been a very, very dangerous thing indeed.

'No, not you,' she said a little breathlessly.

'Then this, perhaps,' Alex suggested, closing the distance between them and taking her in his arms and kissing her, gently at first, almost reverently, and then far more passionately as she swayed closer to him and her heartbeat picked up and echoed the fierce rhythm of the driving rain and her own equally stormy driving inner yearning.

'We should go back,' she protested shakily when Alex released her mouth.

'We can't, it's too late,' he told her, and Beth knew that he wasn't really talking about their actual journey from the castle. 'We *can't* go back, Beth,' he reiterated as he touched her mouth with his fingertips and then traced its trembling shape with his finger. 'Not now...'

'I thought we were going to eat,' Beth reminded him. Her lips felt dry, clumsy, reluctant to form the words, reluctant to do *anything* that would increase the sensual pressure of Alex's fingertips against her lower lip but equally reluctant to deny herself the pleasure of it.

'You're...hungry...?'

The smouldering look which accompanied his comment, the way his gaze dropped from her face to her body, made Beth's heart race.

'I... I...'

'You're right. We *should* eat,' Alex agreed tenderly, reluctantly releasing her. 'Come and sit down by the fire.'

He pulled a chair up for her and Beth allowed him to guide her into it. She wasn't used to being treated so protectively, to being so *cherished*. One part of her loved it, another feared and suspected it. She didn't dare allow herself to fall into the trap of believing that any of this was real, that Alex's treatment of her, his tenderness towards her were genuine. They weren't. She mustn't allow herself to forget that he was simply using her, and that all she felt for him was, quite simply, a healthy physical female desire. She must *not* allow her thoughts or emotions to become clouded by the romanticism of the situation.

Alex picked up the hamper and carried it over to put it down on the floor between them.

'Come and sit down here,' he told her, dragging a couple of soft cushions off the sofa and piling them up against one of the chairs. 'It will be warmer. The chair will protect your back from the draught...'

Obediently Beth did as he suggested. There was something dangerously sybaritic about being here like this with him. The heat from the fire was slowly relaxing her tense muscles whilst the candlelight spread soft, sensuous shadows across the darkening room. Outside the light was already fading, the afternoon giving way to early evening as the storm clouds continued to darken the sky.

'Where did you get this?' Beth asked Alex as he opened the hamper.

'The hotel,' he informed her promptly. 'It's all cold, I'm afraid...'

Beth could have told him that for some reason she was no longer really all that interested in food, but a self-protective instinct made her refrain from doing so. If she did Alex might be tempted to ask just what more compelling appetite had taken its place, and she was very much afraid that she might be tempted to tell him.

'Chicken?' Alex asked her, holding out a tender portion towards her.

Uncertainly Beth looked at it.

'It's good,' Alex encouraged her, taking a bite out of it and then offering it to her, commanding her softly, 'Bite.'

Unable to drag her gaze away from his, Beth did as he instructed, nibbling delicately on the chicken and then tensing as Alex reached out his free hand to push a stray lock of her hair off her face, his fingers just brushing against her mouth as he did so.

There was something almost shockingly sensual about what they were doing, about being fed by him like this, about knowing his fingers were so close to her mouth as he held the chicken and she bit into it, and the temptation to eat the meat with a deliberately erotic female show of the hunger she felt for him was something that Beth had to fight to control.

'Enjoy it,' Alex said softly to her, as though he knew what she was thinking—and feeling. 'An appetite for food is like an appetite for love...meant to be savoured and enjoyed—indulged! That's how I want to make love with you,' he told her rawly.

'Slowly and thoroughly, with every touch, every ca-ress a feast of pleasure and indulgence.'

She was, Beth suddenly discovered, trembling so hard that Alex must be able to see and feel it.

Had Alex brought her here on purpose, to make love to her, to seduce her? If he had…*if* he had, he couldn't have chosen a more romantic setting, Beth acknowledged as Alex threw what was left of the piece of chicken on the fire. Whilst it sizzled in the heat he removed a bottle of wine from the hamper and uncorked it, pouring it into two glasses.

'To us,' he told Beth, handing her one of them and raising his own in a toast.

It was red and full-bodied, and it hit Beth's empty stomach in a warm rich wave that heated her blood, raising her temperature and lowering her resistance.

Having taken another gulp of it, she put down her glass and automatically ran her tongue-tip over her lips. In the firelight she saw Alex's eyes darken fiercely. He held out his own glass to her and told her softly, 'Drink.'

As she bent her head and took a sip he watched her, and then very deliberately and very slowly he turned the glass round, so that the place where she had drunk was facing him, and then equally delib-erately he raised the glass to his own mouth, drinking from exactly the same spot she had drunk from. It was a simple enough gesture, and also a very explicit one. Beth could feel her heat, the response, the awareness, surge through her body in a jagged sen-sation as fierce and primitive as the lightning outside.

'It's *you* I'm thirsting for…hungry for…' Alex told her rawly.

He put down his glass and reached for her, cupping her face as he had done earlier in the day and covering her mouth with his own, his thumb probing the softness of her lower lip, his tongue sliding into the access he had made for it and entwining softly with hers.

And the heat engulfing Beth had nothing whatsoever to do with the fire, nor the sweet film moistening her skin anything to do with the rain hammering down outside.

She *did* try to be strong, to cling to sanity and reason, reminding herself mentally that it was just desire, just sex, a physical appetite—that was all it was, all *he* was. But beneath her fingertips she could feel the heavy thudding of Alex's heart, and Alex himself was urging her to free his body from the restrictive captivity of his clothes, guiding her to buttons and fastenings which, with his help, seemed to come free with almost miraculous speed.

In the firelight his body possessed a magnificence that seemed to echo the feudal ancestry of the castle. He might have been some powerful lord and she a helpless victim of his fiery passion for her, of their *mutually* fiery passion for one another, Beth amended dizzily as she recognised how eager she was for Alex to return the favour she had done him and help her to become free of her own clothes.

Unlike her, though, Alex seemed to need no extra assistance. Beth shivered on the spasm of sharp expectation that gripped her when Alex's hands cupped her naked breasts, her nipples surging excitedly against his palms.

Hot, drenching shudders of excitement raced through her body. Alex was the furnace to which the raw molten material of her desire was drawn.

Slowly Alex removed her clothes, his gaze drinking in the sight of her naked, firelight-washed body. Beth felt as wanton and wild as though she were some long-ago earthy and elemental woman, sure and knowing in her awareness of her own sexuality and desirability.

The pride, the pleasure she felt in her own body as Alex sensuously absorbed the sight, the touch, the scent of her, watching her, stroking his hands over her skin as he shaped her, breathing in what he told her was the unforgettably precious sweet Beth-scent of her, totally banished any self-consciousness or doubt she might have felt.

Here, in the shadowed darkness of this fortress castle which had, over the centuries, seen all the worst and all the best of every human passion, it seemed to Beth everything she felt about herself and about Alex was reduced to its purest and most basic components.

She was a woman; he was a man. She wanted him, ached for him, needed him, and she could see the corresponding intensity of his need for her both in his body and in his eyes.

He might have been her lover returning to her from the heat of battle, their coming together a fierce celebration of the fact that he was still alive; she might have been the virgin bride of the lord of this domain, giving herself to him in a solemn rite of passage.

Before them, in this place, there must have been so many, many earlier lovers, and Beth could almost feel the echoes of their loving echoing the heavy thud of her own heart.

'Have you any idea how much I've wanted to do

this?' Alex groaned as he took hold of her hand, placing it palm to palm against his own, lacing his fingers with hers and then lifting their clasped hands to his mouth whilst he kissed her ring finger.

Against her will Beth felt her own emotional reaction to what he was doing. This was the embodiment of her most private romantic dreams. *This* was how she had always imagined that a lover, her *chosen* lover, would cherish and desire her. A lover who would be both humble and held in thrall to the intensity of his desire for her and yet, too, the master of it, and of her.

'I fell in love with you the first time I saw you,' Alex was telling her huskily.

Love at first sight.

Beth's heart gave a dizzying lurch. It must be the wine that was making her so dangerously tempted to believe him, that was making her *want* to believe him.

'We hardly know one another,' she protested in a whisper.

'I know I want you,' Alex returned. 'I know I love you. I know that your body quivers with pleasure when I touch it so.'

His fingertips trailed liquid fire down her breastbone and over her belly before curling and tugging erotically, gently, on the soft tangle of curls below. As he released them Beth exhaled a long, shaky sigh that ended in a sharp gasp as his fingertip moved lower, finding the delicate cleft of the soft flesh that protected her intimacy. Like the petals of a flower opening to the sure touch of a nectar-seeking bee her body started to respond to his touch.

'And I certainly know what you're doing to me.'

Alex's voice groaned thickly in her ear. 'Feel it, Beth,' he begged her. 'Feel me!'

A little hesitantly at first, but then with growing confidence, Beth spread her hands across his chest, closing her eyes in sensual pleasure as she absorbed the silken heat of his skin. Almost of their own volition her hands moved downwards, beyond the taut arch of Alex's ribcage and over the male flatness of his belly, so masculinely different from hers with its soft curves and sweetly feminine flesh. Very gently, as though just to reassure herself that she hadn't imagined it, Beth moved her hands upwards again, resting her fingertips on the solid rectangle of muscle that formed the male shape of Alex's tough, firm stomach. He wasn't overly muscular, a gym freak whose muscular development was too exaggerated to be truly desirable; he was just right, Beth acknowledged inwardly—perfect...

She hadn't realised she had said the soft, satisfied words of praise out loud until she heard Alex growl and tell her, 'You know traditionally what happens when you praise someone like that, don't you...?'

'Mmm...it makes their head swell,' Beth murmured back absently, and then realised, from what Alex was doing with her hand as he took it and placed it very deliberately and very intimately on his own body, just exactly what he'd meant.

'Mmm...and mine is getting very swollen,' he told her emphatically, although he scarcely needed to make any verbal emphasis of what was now patently obvious to her.

Beneath her fingertips the reality of his body, his maleness, his arousal, made her own flesh quiver excitedly. She wanted him…so much…wanted him… needed him…had to have him…

'Soon…soon…' Alex whispered to her, as though he recognised just what she was feeling.

He kissed her mouth, and then her breasts, gently releasing himself from her hands as he eased her down on the cushions beside the fire. Arching over her naked body in the firelight, he seemed to Beth to be the embodiment of male sexuality, of man himself. He kissed her belly and her muscles quivered, her body quickening as his hands swept downwards, parting her thighs.

Beth had a small mole high up on the inside of one thigh. She saw Alex looking at it, her body tensing as he bent his head and slowly kissed it. Deep inside, the secret female heart of her turned liquid with longing. Very gently Alex reached out to the soft flesh that protected her sex. Beth felt the breath leak painfully from her lungs. Carefully at first, and then more strongly, Alex began to touch her. Excitement exploded through Beth's body as it began to respond rhythmically to Alex's erotic caresses. When his lips and then his tongue started to follow the same path as his fingers Beth moaned a femininely protective protest, but her body's hunger was far, far stronger than any social conditioning or preconceived ideas of female modesty. Nature had already preordained, preprogrammed her body's reaction to what Alex was doing to it.

Beth gasped under the weight of the feelings gathering and coalescing inside her. It was like the climb up towards the highest, most savagely exciting, most dangerous ride she had ever gone on in her whole life. Inexorably she was being pushed towards the top, the summit, her mind and her body tight in panic at the thought of the terrifying freefall into eternity that would come once that summit was crested, even whilst she knew there was nothing she could do to stop it, nothing she *should* do to stop it, urged on as she was by something stronger by far than any mere act of mental will on her part.

Somewhere, someone was moaning: a frantic, keening sound of need that was almost primitive in its intensity. But Beth didn't realise that she was listening to herself until she heard Alex talking to her, soothing her, promising her in between the hot kisses he was pressing all over her naked body that soon he would satisfy her, soon he would fill her, soon he would give them both what they so desperately yearned for.

As he reached her breasts she could feel his hardness pressing down against her body. Her hips writhed hungrily against him, her whole body quickening as he sucked and then bit softly at her nipples. Beth cried out, but not in pain—unless her longing for him could be classed as such. Her whole body trembled, her hips lifting, her legs wrapping possessively around him as Alex stroked her body into eager acceptance of his.

He felt so good, so strong…so right, with her muscles clinging lovingly to him, drawing him deeper and deeper into the soft, welcoming heat of her body.

She heard him groan and cry out a protest that he couldn't wait any longer, that she was too sweet, too hot, too responsive for him to hold back, and then his carefully slow thrusts became an urgent fast-paced rhythm that took him deeper and deeper inside her, carrying them both to the edge of the vortex and

then spectacularly carrying Beth right over and beyond it, to a place where the whole world, the whole
universe dissolved in a physical and emotional display of pyrotechnics that she felt could have rivalled
the birth of the world itself.

Now Beth felt she knew what drove and inspired
the world's greatest artists; now she discovered, quite
simply, she just *knew*.

Alex was holding her in his arms, his heart thudding wildly against hers; her breath was just beginning to slow down, and she wept a little with emotion
as his body slid smoothly from her and he held her
tightly and kissed her.

'Now do you understand just why I love you so
much?' he demanded thickly as he kissed her again,
more slowly and lingeringly.

'This really is the most wonderful fairy-tale place,'
Beth told Alex dreamily. 'It has such a…a special
atmosphere…'

'Mmm…it certainly has,' Alex agreed, with such
a meaningful look at her that Beth could feel her face
starting to burn a little.

'The antiques alone…' She started to babble a little self-consciously, all too well aware that Alex's
prime focus of interest right now was not the castle
or its wonderful furniture, but her…

'Well, if it's antiques you like I shall have to take
you to see my aunt's apartment in Prague. It's the
family's main home and I'd like to take you there,
Beth, introduce you to my family. And besides,
there's something—'

He stopped. Something in his voice made Beth
look a little uncertainly at him, some sense of fore-

boding, of a shadow about to be cast over her blissful haze of happiness.

'My aunt has some of the most wonderful examples of antique crystal in the apartment, and I'm sure she'd be only too pleased to arrange for you to visit the factory and—'

'*No!*'

Beth froze, suddenly wary, suspicion and anger replacing the sensual languor that had had her relaxing into Alex's arms. Now she pulled away from him, all her doubts about him surging back. Julian, too, had used her vulnerability after the kisses they had shared to his own advantage, but Julian had at least stopped at mere kisses. Alex...

'No?'

Alex, too, had withdrawn slightly, and was now frowning. 'But the glass you said you liked in the gift shop is—'

'Impossibly expensive,' Beth snapped sharply at him. 'And besides, I've sourced my own supply at my own price and—'

'You mean the gypsies?' Alex challenged her, his voice now just as sharply critical as her own had been. 'I thought we'd agreed that you weren't going to pursue that...'

Beth tightened her lips in silence and looked away from him, busying herself re-dressing.

'Beth,' Alex said warningly.

'No,' she told him shortly. '*I* agreed nothing. *You* said...'

'So you still intend...' He drew in a swift breath. 'Beth, it's far too dangerous...far too...' He shook his head. 'Believe me, they're leading you on, deceiving you. This factory they've told you about, this mythical source of wonderful glass, is just that. It has to be.

'Look,' he told her softly, leaning towards her and taking hold of her wrists, shaking them gently as though to underline his point, 'there are only a handful of factories that make such glass. I know because my cousins own one of them. It demands a special technique, a special skill…it's…'

'Please let me go,' Beth demanded with stiff formality, her eyes burning with anger and pride as he reluctantly did so. Very deliberately she rubbed her wrists where he had held them, even though in reality they did not actually hurt.

She could see, though, from the dark surge of colour that burned his skin, that he was aware of what she was silently implying, and that she had touched a small raw nerve.

Good! He deserved it.

'I know exactly what you're trying to do, Alex,' she told him crisply. 'I've been there before, you see. Been lied to and deceived by a man who simply wanted to use me for his own ends. I'm not so much of a fool, you know. This is what all this…' she waved her hand around the room and tossed her head scornfully in his direction '…has been all about. You deliberately targeted me, flirted with me…came on to me for the benefit you thought it would bring to your cousins' business, the order you thought you could get. No doubt I'm not your first victim and I doubt that I shall be your last. But where I differ from the others is that *I* saw through you right from the start. You thought you were deceiving me, using me, but in reality I was the one using you.'

'What?'

Beth stood up determinedly as she finished speaking and quickly fastened the rest of her clothes. As he stared at her Alex, too, scrambled to his feet but, oddly, his nudity, instead of rendering him foolish as it might have done another man, only served to remind Beth of exactly how she had felt in his arms, of exactly how he had felt inside her body. Angrily she tried to deny her own inner reaction, to deny what she was feeling emotionally.

'Beth, you couldn't be more wrong,' Alex told her vehemently, 'and I can't understand why you should think…' He gave a short, unamused laugh. 'Believe me, the last thing I would ever do is pimp for business for my cousins. They hardly need it; they have virtually full order books for years to come, if you wish to know…'

Beth smiled loftily and disbelievingly at him.

'That's easy to say now,' she told him cynically. 'You don't fool me, Alex. I've been caught that way before.'

'Beth, you're wrong,' Alex protested stubbornly. 'I love you.' His voice softened and then roughened slightly. 'And I believe that you love me…from the way you loved me just now… If that wasn't love, then just exactly what was it?' He reached out and touched a fingertip to her swollen lips.

'That wasn't love, it was just lust—just sex, that's all,' Beth interrupted him scornfully.

'Just sex?'

'Just sex,' Beth confirmed firmly. Why was the look in his eyes making something hurt so much deep inside her chest? He didn't really care about her. She'd be a fool if she started believing that he did. He was another Julian, just out for what he could get.

'I know exactly what's going on, Alex,' she told him coolly. 'Your cousins pay you to put as much new business their way as you can.' She gave a small shrug. 'I can't blame you for trying to push me into buying from them, I suppose, but what I *can* do is make it plain to you that it's a ploy I'm simply not going to fall for. I may have been a gullible little fool in the past, but I'm not any more.'

'I understand,' Alex told her gently. 'Another man has hurt you badly. I'd like to kill him for it, but more than that I'd like to take the pain away for you, Beth. I'd like to love you whole and happy again. Do you still love him?'

'Julian Cox?' Beth looked scathing. 'No, the man I *thought* I loved, the man I thought loved me, never really existed. Julian was like you. He just wanted what he could get out of me financially. Fortunately for me, though, unlike you, he wasn't prepared to use sex to get it.'

'You weren't lovers?' Alex asked her swiftly.

'You and I aren't *lovers*,' Beth couldn't resist telling him. 'We just had sex. And, no, Julian and I didn't have sex. I suppose part of the reason I wanted you was because I was just quite simply sexually frustrated,' she told Alex carelessly, with a small dismissive shrug, before adding musingly, 'Perhaps I should give your cousins a small order after all. You were very…thorough…'

Beth knew that she was behaving outrageously, but something was driving her on, forcing her to do so. Some protective, deep-rooted instinct for self-preservation was warning her that she must use every means she could to keep Alex at bay emotionally, to make sure that there was an unbridgeable distance between them.

'My God, if I thought you actually meant that—' Alex swore savagely.

'I do mean it,' Beth fibbed, tilting her head defiantly.

'So you *don't* love me?' Alex demanded quietly.

'No. No, I don't love you,' Beth agreed in a slightly tremulous voice.

There was a long, deathly silence and then Alex said bleakly, 'I see…'

He started to get dressed, and without looking at her he continued, 'In that case I'd better drive you back to Prague.'

'Yes, I think that would be a good idea,' Beth agreed.

CHAPTER EIGHT

'WHAT are you looking at?'

Alex didn't move as his mother raised herself up on her tiptoes and looked over his shoulder at the photograph he was studying. Her face became sad and shadowed as she recognised it.

'You still feel the same way about her.'

It was a statement, not a question, and Alex simply nodded as he replaced the photograph he had taken of Beth in Prague back in his wallet.

'Oh, Alex, I'm so sorry,' his mother sympathised.

'Not half so sorry as I am,' Alex told her dryly.

Alex's mother had heard the full story about her son's meeting with Beth in Prague and the events that had followed it from Alex himself, after he had returned home to England to take up a new appointment as the Chair of Modern History at a local university. It was a prestigious appointment, and one she felt her cherished only child entirely merited, but it had soon become plain to her that Alex was far from happy. When questioned he had grimly explained to her that he had fallen in love with a girl who had not returned his feelings, a statement which had aroused all his mother's protective maternal instincts. How could *any* woman not love her *wonderful* son?

In any other circumstances Alex would have been amused by her reaction. His mother was neither possessive nor clinging, quite the opposite, and she had taught him to value his independence as she and his father valued theirs. Loving someone meant allowing them the right to choose their own way of life, she had always told him. One thing Alex had not told her, though, was that he and Beth had been lovers— or rather, as Beth had so clinically put it, had had sex. That was something that was far too private to be discussed with anyone. The truth was that Beth might only have had sex with him, but he had quite definitely made love with her. Made love, and put love, his heart and soul, his whole self, into every kiss, every touch, every caress he had given her.

Even now he could hardly believe the accusations she had made against him. The day after he had left her at the hotel following their return from the castle he had gone to see her, only to discover that she had checked out of the hotel without leaving a forwarding address.

It had been some time before he had been able to return home, and he had lost count of the number of occasions he had been tempted to get in his car and drive to Rye-on-Averton to see her, to demand an explanation…to beg for a second chance. But on each occasion his pride and his self-respect had stopped him. If she didn't love him then he had no right to try and compel her to accept him. But how could she have responded to him the way she had if she did not love him?

'Lucy Withers' daughter is back from Greece. She really is the most pretty girl. I saw her the other night when I called round to see Lucy. Do you remember the way she used to follow you around?'

Alex shook his head.

'Nice try, Ma, but I'm afraid it isn't going to work.

You can't stop a haemorrhaging artery with a sticking plaster,' he told her grimly.

'Why don't you go and see Beth…talk to her…?' his mother urged him softly.

Alex shook his head.

'There wouldn't be any point.'

He couldn't tell her that to do so would, in his eyes at least, be tantamount to forcing himself on Beth, and besides, he didn't think he could face the look in her eyes when she told him she didn't want him. He still woke up in the night, his body tensing in denial as he relived the first time. To go from the heights he had believed they had both reached to the depths of despair he had felt when she had told him that she didn't love him had been too much to endure at one gulp.

'Well, you know best,' his mother told him, and then added, 'Oh, I nearly forgot to tell you—your aunt telephoned. The authorities have released the stolen glassware back to them at long last. You know they were told that it had been recovered but the police wouldn't tell them anything else?'

Alex nodded.

'Well, it turns out that it had been stolen on the orders of a gang of criminals who were using it as bait to draw in unwary foreign buyers. They promised them glass of a similar quality as a means of getting their hands on foreign currency, but in reality fulfilled the orders they took with the very poorest quality, cheap stuff. The whole thing only came to light when customers started complaining to their own embassies about the orders they had received—

'Alex! *Alex!* Where on earth are you going?' his

mother demanded as Alex suddenly started to stride towards the door.

'Alex,' she protested, but her son wasn't listening.

His mind working overtime, Alex hurried out to his car. As he swung his powerful BMW into the main stream of traffic his thoughts were busy.

Supposing Beth *had* been caught in this scam his mother had just described to him?

He didn't live very far away from his parents—less than fifteen minutes' drive. He soon pulled into the driveway to the large Edwardian mansion where he owned a handsome ground-floor apartment.

'Alex, it's beautiful!' his mother had exclaimed the first time he had shown it to her. 'But it's far too large for a single man.' She had looked hopefully at him, but he had shaken his head.

'I like my home comforts and my own space,' he had told her, but what he had *not* told her was that when he had been viewing the apartment what had clinched the quick sale for him had been the resemblance of the drawing room to the salon at the castle where he and Beth had made love.

There had been many times since he had bought it when he had looked into the flickering flames of the fire and wondered if he was crazy to torment himself the way he was doing…many, many times when he had had his hand on the receiver to dial the number of a builder to come and take the fireplace out. And then he had looked into the flames and remembered the way he had seen the firelight flickering shadows on Beth's body what seemed now like a lifetime ago, and he just hadn't been able to make the call.

There was no need for him to pack anything—Rye-on-Averton wasn't that far away.

Half an hour later, as he swung his big car out onto the motorway slip road, it was as though he had already driven the route before, and in his thoughts he already had.

This wasn't mere indulgence of his own needs and feelings, he assured himself as the powerful car ate up the miles. This was a duty, an almost sacred charge. An act of responsibility, an act of faith…an act of love.

White-faced, Beth replaced her telephone receiver. She had spent most of the morning on the telephone, and the call she had just received from the Board of Trade had confirmed what she had already begun to fear. The factory…her factory…simply did not exist. She had been conned…cheated…

Beth sat down on the floor of the storeroom and covered her face with her hands. What on earth was she going to do? It was bad enough that she had wasted all this time reliving what had happened in Prague with Alex, reminding herself of…of things she just did not want to remember: the silent drive back to Prague, her decision the moment she reached the hotel to find somewhere else to stay, just in case Alex refused to accept what she had told him and just in case she weakened…just in case her emotions weren't as uninvolved as she had claimed…

Then there had been her visit to the factory with the gypsy: the peculiar silence of the factory itself, the ramshackle untidiness of it, the overgrown car park, and then the oddly sumptuous office, with its dirty faded wallpaper and its completely contrasting heavily locked cabinets filled with that beautiful glass.

Beth winced as she remembered how nearly she had backed out of giving them an order when she had been told just how much glass she would have to take.

'That's far too much,' she had protested. 'I can't afford to buy so much.'

In the end they had agreed that she could divide the order into the four different colours of glass, but she had still needed to go back to her new hotel and ring home, to persuade her bank manager to increase her overdraft facility.

'I can't increase it to that level,' he had protested. 'The business doesn't merit it. You don't have the security.'

Beth had thought frantically.

'I have some security,' she had told him, and it was true; she'd had the shares her grandfather had given her for her twenty-first birthday and an insurance policy that was supposed to be the basis for her pension. In the end her bank manager had agreed to lend her the money, secured by these assets.

She had returned home from Prague, jubilant at having succeeded in securing the order—and on her own terms. But her jubilation had been short-lived—rootless, really—and underneath it there had been a vast subterranean cavern of pain and loss which she had fought valiantly but hopelessly to deny.

'It was just lust—just sex, that's all,' she had told Alex, but she had lied... Oh, how she had lied...to herself as well as to him. The tears on her face when she woke from her longing dreams of him and for him told her that much.

'I love you,' he had told her, but she knew he hadn't meant it.

'I don't love you,' she had said, and she certainly hadn't meant that.

How was it possible for her to have fallen in love with him after all she had done to try to protect herself, all she had told herself…warned herself…? Beth had no idea, and in the weeks following her return she had been too exhausted by the pain of keeping her feelings at bay, too driven by the fear of what was happening to her, to look too deeply into the whys and wherefores of what had happened. It was enough, more than enough, just to know that it had. To know it and to bitterly, bitterly wish that she did not.

The only thing that had kept her going had been the thought of her glass, her precious, wonderful glass, and now, like the love Alex had claimed he felt for her, that too had revealed itself to be false and worthless.

Her telephone rang and she tensed. Twice since her return home she had received calls from Prague. On one occasion it had been the hotel, telephoning about a scarf she had left behind, and the second time it had been an anonymous caller who had rung off when she'd answered the phone.

'Alex, Alex,' she had cried out frantically, but she had been simply crying into silence.

'Beth, it's Dee…' her landlady announced at the other end of the line. 'Is it unpacked yet? Can I come round?'

Immediately Beth panicked.

'No. No…'

'Is something wrong?'

Beth bit her lip. Dee was too quick, too intelligent to be fobbed off with a lie.

'Well, actually, yes…there is,' she admitted. 'The order isn't—'

'They've sent you the wrong order?' Dee interrupted before Beth could finish. 'You must get in touch with them immediately, Beth, and insist that they ship the correct one, at their own expense and express. Tell them that if they don't you'll be submitting a claim to them for loss of business. Did you stipulate on your contract that the order had to be delivered in time for your Christmas market? I know they've already delayed delivery several times.'

'I…I have to go, Dee,' Beth fibbed. 'There's another call coming through.'

What on earth was she going to do? How was she going to explain to Kelly, her partner, that because of her…her stupidity…they were probably going to have to close the shop? How could they keep it open when they didn't have anything to sell? How could they continue to pay their overheads when they had no money? She had already received one letter from the bank, reminding her that they were expecting her overdraft to be repaid just as soon as Christmas was over.

There was no way she was going to be able to do that now. She knew, of course, that Brough, Kelly's husband, was an extremely wealthy man, and no doubt he would be prepared to help them out, but her pride wouldn't allow her to be a party to that. And besides, Brough was essentially a businessman, and Beth was under no illusions about what he was likely to think of her business capabilities once he knew what had happened.

Was she *never* going to get a thing right? Was she *always* going to be taken for a fool…was she always going to *be* a fool?

It was all too much…much too much. Beth bowed her head. She couldn't cry. She was beyond that—way, way beyond the easy relief of tears—and besides, she had cried so many times since her return from Prague.

Only now, when she had reached the very bottom of her personal hell, could she truly admit to herself just how deeply she had fallen in love with Alex…how much she missed him…ached for him…

Alex found Beth's shop without any difficulty. It was, after all, on the main shopping street of the small town. He parked his car and got out, walking towards the elegant three-storey building and pausing to study the attractively set out window for a few seconds. There was no sign of anyone inside the shop, although the sign had been turned to 'open'. He hesitated for a few seconds, and then pushed open the door.

Beth heard the shop doorbell ring and called through the half-open storeroom door, 'I'll be with you in a second.'

Beth—Beth was here. Alex closed the shop door and swiftly turned, striding towards the open stockroom door.

Beth was just getting to her feet as he walked in. The blood left her face as she saw him, and for a moment she actually thought that she was going to faint.

'Alex…you…what…what are you doing here?' she whispered painfully, her eyes huge with the intensity of her shock.

Alex hardly dared to look at her.

The moment he had heard her voice, never mind seen her, he had been filled with such a need, such a hunger that he'd had to clench his hands into fists and stuff them into his pockets to prevent himself from taking hold of her.

As she saw the way Alex was avoiding looking at her, focusing instead on the untidy disarray of the half-unpacked packing cases in the storeroom, Beth knew immediately why he had come. The breathtaking cruelty of it stabbed right through her.

She saw him look at the crude unsaleable items of her order which she had already unpacked, and then, for the first time, he looked directly at her, with an expression in his eyes which she immediately interpreted as a mixture of distaste and pity.

Immediately her hackles rose defensively. Immediately she knew exactly what he was doing, that he had come to crow over her, to mock and taunt her, to tell her 'I told you so'. The fact that her thought processes might be a little illogical didn't occur to her; her emotions were far too aroused and overwrought for any kind of analytical thought.

'You *knew*, didn't you? Didn't you?' she challenged him bitterly. 'You've come to laugh at me…to *gloat*…'

'Beth, you're wrong…'

'Yes, I am,' she agreed emotionally. 'I'm always wrong. Always… I was wrong about Julian. I thought *he* loved me. I was wrong about you. I thought…I thought that at least you'd have the decency not to…' She stopped and swallowed, and then added wretchedly, 'And I was wrong about the glass as well.' Her head lifted proudly.

'Well, then, go ahead, say it… ''I told you so…'''
Her mouth twisted in a pitiful facsimile of a smile. 'At least I won't be making the same mistake a second time…'

Somehow she managed to force back the tears she could feel threatening her composure.

One look at the semi-unpacked crates and what they contained had confirmed Alex's very worst fears. The order she had received was wholly worthless, totally unsaleable. He ached for her as he compared what she had received to the glass produced by his cousins: fine, first-quality, beautiful stemware that richly echoed all the tradition and purity of the antique designs they still faithfully adhered to. Copies, yes, but beautiful ones, expensive ones, Alex acknowledged, as he remembered how awed his mother had been the first time she had visited Prague and the family business.

'They sell their glassware all over the world. Japan, America, the Gulf States. It is beautiful, Alex, but, oh, it's so expensive. Your cousins gave me these,' she had added reverently, unpacking the set of a dozen wine glasses which had been the family's gift to her.

'Are you insured against…this kind of risk?' Alex asked Beth gently, but he already knew the answer and didn't need the brief shake of her head to tell him that she wasn't. Compassion and love filled his eyes. He looked away from her.

'The Czech authorities have tracked down the criminals who organised this. Ultimately there will be a court case…perhaps there may even be some form of compensation for…for you…' he suggested.

Beth looked briefly at him.

'Don't treat me like a child, Alex. Of course there won't be any compensation. Why should I be compensated for being a fool? And even if there was…it would be too little too late,' she added hollowly.

'What do you mean?' Alex pounced.

'I…I don't mean anything,' Beth denied quickly, but she could tell that he didn't believe her.

'Beth, are you there?'

Beth tensed as she heard Dee's voice.

'I thought I'd come down. You didn't sound very happy when I spoke to you on the phone. If there's a problem with this glass… Oh!'

Dee stopped speaking as she walked into the storeroom and realised that Beth wasn't alone—and then she saw the glass.

Beth winced as she saw Dee's horrified expression.

'What on earth…?' Dee began, and then stopped. 'I'm sorry, Beth,' she apologised, 'but…'

Alex acted quickly. His mind had been working overtime and he had come to an impulsive and probably very unwise decision but he simply couldn't bear to see the shame and pain in his darling Beth's eyes.

'Yes, you're quite right,' he told Beth, as much to her confusion as Dee's. 'The order will have to be replaced.'

'It most certainly will,' Dee agreed swiftly, turning to Alex with, 'And in time for the Christmas market.'

'Dee…' Beth began, knowing that she would have to tell Dee the truth—that not only was Alex not responsible for her order, but also that there was no way he could correct the mistake she herself had made. Not in time for the Christmas market and, in fact, not ever. She would also have to tell Dee that she was going to have to terminate her lease, but that was something that would have to wait until after she had spoken to Kelly—and the bank.

Right now, what she wanted more than anything else was to close her eyes and transport herself back to a time before she had gone to Prague, before she had ever met Alex, before she had ever known Julian…before…

'If you'll excuse us,' Alex was saying affably but firmly to Dee, 'I think this is something Beth and I need to discuss in private.'

'Beth?' Dee began questioningly, and Beth nodded. What other option did she really have?

'Er…yes…it's all right… I'll be fine,' she reassured Dee, knowing what the other woman was thinking.

Just as soon as Beth had heard the shop door close behind Dee she turned on Alex and demanded tiredly, 'What did you say that for, about the order being replaced? You know it isn't true.'

Her voice cracked as the real emotion generating her anger surfaced and betrayed her.

'Beth. Beth, please don't,' Alex begged her, feeling her pain as though it was his own and aching to make things right for her. 'Look, is there somewhere we can go to talk in private?' he asked her.

'I don't want to talk to you. There isn't anything more you can say,' Beth told him bitterly. 'You've done what you came to do…had your gloat. You should be satisfied with that.'

But Alex shook his head.

'You've got it wrong. That isn't why I'm here. Look, why don't I close the shop and we can talk in here and…?'

'No, not here,' Beth denied, shivering slightly as she looked round at the packing cases. She couldn't bear to spend another minute in here with them, with the evidence of her stupidity.

'I live upstairs…it's this way…'

'Let's lock the shop door first,' Alex suggested gently. Beth's face burned. She should have been the one to think of that. Where was her sense of responsibility, her maturity, her…? She tensed as Alex came back.

'I've put the "closed" sign up and locked the door,' he told her.

Silently Beth led the way to the rear door; just as silently Alex followed her.

Why had Alex said that to Dee about the glassware being replaced when they both knew that was impossible? What on earth was Dee going to think when Beth had to tell her that Alex had lied and that she had let him?

Once they were in her sitting room Beth stood defensively behind one of the chairs, indicating to Alex that he should take a seat in the other one.

'Beth, I promise you that I didn't come here to gloat,' he told her, ignoring the chair and coming instead to stand in front of her.

'Then why did you come?' Beth demanded. He was standing far too close to her, the chair between them no defence at all to the way her body was reacting to him, and certainly no defence against the emotional bombardment his presence was inflicting on her senses.

Even without closing her eyes she was sharply, shockingly aware of just how he would look without his clothes, of just how he would feel…smell…be…

A small keening noise bubbled in her throat. Frantically she fought to suppress it.

'I came because…because…I wanted to warn you just in case you hadn't actually paid for the glass already,' Alex prevaricated. It was, after all, partially true. That was certainly what had urged him into action, even if the real reasons for what he had done were far more complex and personal.

'How…how did you know, anyway…about… about the glass?'

She was, Beth discovered, finding it very difficult to concentrate on what she was trying to say. Alex's proximity was distracting and dizzying her. It would be so easy just to reach out and touch him. All she had to do was to lean forward a little and raise her hand and then she would…she could… Despairingly she moistened her dry lips with the tip of her tongue.

Hurriedly Alex looked away from her. If she kept on touching her mouth like that there was no way he was going to be able to stop himself from taking hold of her.

He tried to concentrate on what she was asking him.

'I…er…my mother told me. The glass you were originally shown was stolen from my cousins. The thieves were using it to lure unsuspecting buyers into placing orders for what they believed would be good-quality reproduction glassware like the items they had been shown—items which were, in fact, genuine antiques—and I—'

'So it wasn't just me...I wasn't the only...?'

'The only one? No, not by a long chalk,' Alex reassured her.

'The only fool,' Beth had been about to say, and she was sure that was what Alex must privately consider her to be. Now that he had told her she couldn't understand how she had ever believed the glassware she had been shown was modern. Perhaps she had believed it because she had *wanted* to believe it.

'Your cousins must be pleased to have recovered their antiques,' Beth told Alex tonelessly.

'Yes, especially my aunt. She felt the most responsible because she was the one who had resisted installing a new alarm system.'

'Did the night-watchman recover from his injuries?' Beth asked Alex suddenly, remembering how he had told her about the burglary the day he had taken her to see the castle.

'Yes. Yes, he did,' Alex confirmed, looking surprised that she had remembered such a small detail of their conversation. Beth looked away from him. She could recall virtually everything he had ever said to her, and everything he had ever done.

'Are you...are you back in England permanently now?'

'Yes...yes, I had my year out and now I've accepted a Chair at Lexminster, lecturing in Modern History.'

Beth stared at him white-faced. There was no mistaking the reality of what he was telling her, nor its truth. She might have doubted him originally when he had told her he was a university lecturer, but now, listening to the calm way he was discussing his career, she knew he had spoken the truth. She was the one who had been guilty of deceit, not him—she had wilfully deceived herself about her real feelings for him, her real reason for feeling those feelings. A sharp pain twisted through her heart. She could just imagine how attractive his female students would find him, how easily they would probably fall in love with him…as easily as she herself had done.

'Beth, about this glass. Let me speak to my family,' he began, but Beth shook her head quickly.

'I know what you're trying to do but it's no good,' she informed him tersely. 'I just don't have the money to place another order, Alex—not with your cousins, not with anyone. In fact—' she lifted her head and looked proudly at him '—when you arrived I was just about to get in touch with my partner to tell her that we're going to have to close the business down. I owe the bank too much to continue.

'Why aren't you telling me that it serves me right, that I should have listened to you in the first place?' Beth asked him painfully in the silence that followed her disclosure.

'Oh, Beth…'

Tenderly Alex closed the distance between them, reaching past the chair to take her in his arms and cradle her against his body, whispering soft words of endearment in her ear, kissing the top of her head and then her closed eyelids, her cheekbones, the tip of her nose…her lips…

'Alex… No…no…'

Frantically Beth tore herself out of his arms.

'I want you to go. I want you to go *now*,' she told him shakily.

'Beth,' Alex protested, but Beth didn't dare allow herself to listen to him.

'Very well. If you won't leave then I shall have to,' she told him, starting to hurry towards the door.

'Beth, Beth, it's all right. I'll go. I'm going,' Alex told her soothingly.

Beth didn't look at him as she heard him walking past her towards the door. It hurt so much more to know he was leaving her life this time. Before, in Prague, she had been so angry that that had protected her to some extent from the reality of her pain. The knowledge of how she really felt about him had only come later, after the heat of her anger had died. But now she had no anger to protect her. Now there was no barrier between her and the pain.

Impulsively she hurried to her sitting-room window. Alex was just getting into his car, and Beth's eyes widened as she realised how expensive and up-market it was. Oddly, despite his casual clothes, the car seemed to suit him. In fact, Beth recognised, on a fresh stab of pain, Alex was carrying about him a very distinctive air of authority. Even in Prague she had been aware that he was quite a bit older and more mature than the majority of the young students taking their gap year out between finishing university and finding a job, but now, seeing him on her own home ground, she was struck by how easily he would fit into the same mould as Kelly's Brough and Anna's even more formidably successful husband Ward.

Alex was starting his car. Beth leaned closer to the window, yearning for one last glimpse of him. As though he sensed that she was watching him he looked back towards the window where she was standing. Immediately Beth drew away from it, pain drowning out all the voices of rationality that tried to tell her that she had done the right thing, that all he had really come for had been to taunt her and gloat over her, that he had lied to her when he had claimed to be concerned.

Half an hour later Beth was just on her way back down to the shop when she caught sight of the wedding invitation she had placed on the sitting-room mantelpiece. Dee's cousin Harry was marrying Brough's sister Eve the week before Christmas, and Beth had been invited to the ceremony.

A wedding. The celebration of two people's love for one another.

Betrayingly Beth's eyes filled with acidly hot tears.

'I fell in love with you the first time I saw you,' Alex had told her, but of course he hadn't meant it. Of course he had lied to her.

She had known that then. She knew it now. So why was she crying?

CHAPTER NINE

BETH sat staring into space, nursing a mug of coffee. She had just closed the shop for the day. It was almost a week since she had received her Czech order, and five days since she had seen Alex. Five days, three hours and…she glanced at the kitchen clock…eighteen minutes.

Kelly was away now with Brough, and Beth wanted to wait until after she had returned home before she told her the bad news about the business. She still had to speak with the bank manager as well. She got up wearily.

She was tired of explaining to eager customers that there had been a mistake with the Czech order and that the glass hadn't arrived. She had repacked the cases, but of course there was no point in trying to return them to an empty factory.

A car boot sale might be her best chance of getting rid of them—provided she was prepared to pay people to take the stuff, she decided with grimly bitter humour.

After washing her mug she went back downstairs to the shop. Some of the Christmas novelties she had ordered earlier in the year at a trade fair had arrived and had to be unpacked. Although pretty enough in their way, they could not possibly compare with what she had hoped to be displaying.

She had *some* good stock to sell—items she had bought prior to her visit to Prague. Ordinarily Beth had a good eye for colour, and a very definite flair for the placement of things. In the window she had a display of fluted iridescent pinky-gold fine glass candle-holders and stemmed dishes, on one of which she had piled high shimmering pastel glass sweets. It looked very effective, and she had seen several people stop for a closer look.

Admiring it as she walked past their small cubbyhole of an office, she could hear the fax clattering. She grimaced to herself as she went to see what was happening. It was probably a message from her mother. Beth was going home to spend Christmas with her family and her mother was constantly sending her shopping lists of things she wanted Beth to buy on her behalf.

Absently Beth glanced at the machine, and then tensed, quickly re-reading the message it was printing.

The Glass Factory, Prague, to Ms Bethany Russell.
Re your order.
We have pleasure to confirm that your order for four dozen each of our special Venetian cut-glass stemware in colours ruby, madonna, emerald and gold is now completed and will be despatched immediately, air freight, to arrive Manchester, England...

Beth ripped the paper out of the machine, her hands shaking. What was going on? She hadn't ordered any glass. How could she? She couldn't afford to.

She reached for the fax machine, her eyes on the

number printed on the message she had just received, and then she stopped.

'Beth…?'

She hurried out of the office as she heard Dee's voice, the fax still in her hand.

'Have you heard anything about your glass yet?' Dee asked her, and then, glancing at the fax message, added, 'Oh, yes, I can see you have…they're sending you a fresh order. Well, I should think so too. When will it arrive? I'll come with you to the airport to collect it, if you like.'

'Dee, I haven't—'

'You're going to need to get it unpacked and on display as soon as it arrives. I'll come and give you a hand.

'Oh, and by the way, you know that man who was here when I came in the other day? Why didn't you tell me who he was…'

'Who he was…?' Beth repeated dully. 'I…'

'Mmm…I had to go over to Lexminster at the weekend—an old friend of my father's lives there, and of course I was at university there myself. He used to be a professor at the university and still attends some of the functions. He insisted on my accompanying him to a drinks party at one of the colleges and your friend was there.'

'Alex?' Beth questioned her. 'Alex was there?'

'Mmm…he was explaining to me about his family connections with Prague, and he did say, too, that he had told them how imperative it was that you got your order just as quickly as possible.'

'Dee, please…' Beth began. She would have to tell Dee the truth.

'I can't stay, I'm afraid.' Dee overrode her. 'I only

popped in to see how you were. I've got a meeting in less than an hour. We'll go out for supper next week, but remember to ring me as soon as your order arrives…'

As she got in her car to drive away Dee was conscious of an unfamiliar heat burning her face. She glanced in her driving mirror, anxious to see if she looked as uncomfortably self-conscious as she felt. As a young teenager she had endured the misery of a particularly painful blush which it had taken her a lot of effort to learn to control.

In fact, those who knew her now would no doubt be surprised to learn just how shy and awkward she had felt as a young girl.

All that was behind her now. Her father's death had propelled her into adulthood with a speed and a force that had left its mark on her almost as much as losing him had. The pain and anguish of those dark days still sometimes haunted her, no matter how hard she tried not to let them.

Going back to her old university hadn't helped, and the relief she had experienced at seeing even a vaguely familiar face at the cocktail party she had so reluctantly agreed to attend had negated her normal sense of curiosity, so that she hadn't really asked very many questions of Alex Andrews, although she had noted how keen he had been to talk about Beth.

It had been her father's old friend who had brought up the subject of Julian Cox, though, asking, 'Do you see anything of that Cox fellow these days?' and then shaking his head before opining, 'He was a bad lot, if you ask me. Your father…'

Anxious not to reactivate painful memories for either of them, Dee had quickly tried to change the subject, but Alex Andrews, who had been standing with them at the time, had frowned and joined the conversation, asking her, 'Julian Cox? That would be the man who Beth…?'

'Yes. Yes…' Dee had confirmed quickly. If she had to talk about Julian, she would much rather the conversation centred on Beth's relationship with him rather than her own or her father's. She knew that people thought of her as being cool and controlled. Outwardly maybe she was. But inside—no one knew just how difficult she found it sometimes not to give way to her emotions, not to betray her real feelings.

'He hurt her very badly,' Alex had said curtly.

'Yes, he did,' Dee had agreed. 'We…her friends…thought at one point that…' She'd paused and shaken her head. 'That was one of the reasons we encouraged her to go to Prague. We thought it might help to take her mind off Julian. As it happens, though, her feelings weren't as deeply involved as either we or she had feared. I think once Beth realised just what kind of man he was she recognised how worthless he was, and how impossible it was for her to really care about him.

'She obviously spoke to you about him,' she had added curiously.

'She told me that because of him she found it impossible to trust any man…not in those words, perhaps, but that was certainly the message she wanted to give me.'

'Julian is an expert at destroying people's trust,' Dee had told him, looking away as she did so so that he wouldn't see the shadow darkening her eyes.

They had gone their separate ways shortly after

that. There had been several old colleagues her father's friend had wanted to talk with, and Dee had good-naturedly accompanied him, joining in their conversations even though there hadn't been one of them under seventy years of age and the people and events they were discussing had had little relevance for her.

Mind you, in many ways it was just as well that she hadn't needed to concentrate too hard on what was being said. That had left her free to keep a weather eye on the room, strategically placing herself so that she had a clear view of the entrance. She hadn't wanted to be caught off guard by the arrival of…of…anyone—

Sternly now, Dee reminded herself that she had an important meeting to attend, and that she needed to keep her wits about her if she was to keep the two warring factions on her action committee from falling out with one another.

A little ruefully she reflected on how something so therapeutic and 'green' as planting a new grove of English trees on a piece of land recently bought in a joint enterprise between the local council and one of her charities could arouse such warrior-like feelings amongst her committee members. Her father would have known exactly how to handle the situation, of course, and it was at times like these that she missed him the most. Chatting with his contemporaries, she had been so sharply aware of her loss, and not just of the father she had loved so much. Had he lived, what might she have been now? A wife…a mother…?

Dee swallowed quickly. She could still become a mother if that was her ambition. These days one did not even need to have a lover to achieve the ambition, never mind a partner. But she had been brought up by a sole parent herself, and, much as she had loved her father, much as he had loved her, she had missed not having a mother.

How often as a young girl had she dreamed of being part of a large family of brothers and sisters, and two parents? She had had her aunts and uncles and her cousins, it was true, but…

Her agents had still not been able to find out what had happened to Julian after he had disappeared to Singapore.

Dee moved uncomfortably in her seat. The cocktail party had reawakened old memories, old heartache and pain, old wounds which had healed with a dangerously thin and fragile new skin.

Alex smiled warmly as he heard his aunt's voice on the other end of the telephone line.

'How are you?'

'Tired,' his aunt told him wryly. 'It's meant hard work, getting this important order together for you.'

Beth was just about to close up the shop for the night when she saw the delivery van pull up outside, followed by a highly polished chauffeur-driven black Mercedes.

It had been raining during the afternoon and the pavements were wet, glistening under the light from the Christmas decorations which the Corporation's workmen had been putting up and which they were currently testing, prior to the formal switching-on ceremony the following weekend.

On the counter in front of her Beth had a list of

customers she intended to ring during the evening. They were the customers who had expressed an interest in the new glass. She had not, as yet, told them that it wasn't going to be available.

The van driver was heading towards her door. Uncertainly Beth watched him, her uncertainty turning to shock as she saw the woman climbing out of the rear of the elegant Mercedes and recognised her instantly.

It was Alex's aunt, the woman she had seen him with in Prague, looking, if anything, even more soignée and elegant now than she had done then. The exquisite tailoring of her charcoal-grey suit made Beth sigh in soft envy. If she had only added a picture hat and a small toy dog on a lead she could have posed for a Dior advertisement of the fifties. Very few women of her own generation could boast of having such a lovely neat waist, Beth acknowledged as Alex's aunt waited for the van driver to open the shop door and then stand back, allowing Alex's aunt to sweep through.

'This is very good,' she told Beth without preamble. 'Alex told me that you had a good eye and I can see that he is right. That is a very pretty display of pieces you have in your window, although perhaps you might just redirect the spotlight on them a little. If you have some ladders I could perhaps show you...'

Beth was too bemused to feel affronted, and besides, she had come to very much the same decision herself only this afternoon.

'I have brought you your glass,' she added, and then said more severely, 'I hope you understand that we do this only as the very greatest favour because it is for family. It has been very expensive to pay the workpeople to work extra and push your order through. I have a rich—a very rich—oil sheikh who right at this moment has had to be told that his chandelier is not quite ready. This is not something I would normally like to do, but Alex was most insistent, and when a man is so much in love…'

She gave a graceful shrug of her shoulders.

'I have come here with it myself since we do not normally sell our glassware to enterprises such as yours. We sell, normally, by personal recommendation, direct to our customers. That is our…our speciality. We do not…how would you say?…make so much that it can be sold as in a supermarket.' She gave another dismissive shrug. 'That is not our way. We are unique and…exclusive.'

'Yes, you may put them here,' she instructed the van driver, who was wheeling in a large container. 'But carefully, carefully…

'Oh, yes, I thank you. I nearly forgot…' She thanked the chauffeur as he followed the van driver in and handed her a large rectangular gift-wrapped package.

'This is for you,' she told Beth, to Beth's astonishment. 'You will not open it yet. That is not permitted. You will open it with Alex—he will have one too—when you are together. It is a gift of betrothal—a tradition in our family.'

Betrothal!

Beth stared at her. Alex's aunt was so very much larger than life, so totally compelling that Beth felt completely overwhelmed by her. By rights she ought to be telling her that there was no way she could accept the order she had just brought. She just couldn't afford it. And she should also tell her that she resented Alex's high-handed attitude in giving his family an order on her behalf without consulting her in the first place. And as for his aunt's comment about a betrothal...

'It is also very much a tradition that the men of our family fall in love at first sight. My husband, who was also my second cousin, fell in love with me just by seeing my photograph. One glimpse, that was all it took, and then he was on his way to my parents' home to beg me to be his wife. We were together as man and wife for just two years and then he was killed...murdered...'

Beth gave a small convulsive shiver as she saw the look in the older woman's eyes.

'I still feel the pain of his loss today. It has been my life's work to do with the factory what he would have wished to be done. One of my greatest sorrows is that he did not live to see our family reunited. Alex is very much like him. He loves you. You are very lucky to have the love of such a man,' she told Beth firmly.

Beth simply had no idea what on earth to say to her, much less how to tell her that she had got it all wrong, that Alex most certainly did not love her.

'This is good,' she informed the van driver, who had now brought in what Beth sincerely hoped was the last packing case. There were six of them in all, filling her small shop, and she dreaded to think what the cost of their contents must be. Quite definitely much, much more than she could afford, with her empty bank account and her burdensome overdraft.

'I really don't think...' she began faintly. But trying to stop Alex's aunt was like trying to stop the awesome magnificence of some grandly rolling river at full flood—impossible!

'You will please remove the covering,' Alex's aunt was instructing the van driver, waving one elegantly manicured hand in the direction of the boxes.

Beth didn't dare look at him. This was an egalitarian age, an age of equality in which, Beth suspected, the last time a man had removed something from its packing for *her* had been when her father had opened her last babyhood Easter egg. But to her astonishment, far from reacting with the surly resentment she had expected to Alex's aunt's request, the van driver immediately, enthusiastically complied. Beth acknowledged the uneasy suspicion crowding her already log-jammed thoughts: he must have been promised an extremely generous tip indeed.

'No. No more,' Alex's aunt commanded, once the lids were removed and the van driver was about to delve into the polystyrene chips surrounding the contents.

'First we must have champagne,' she told Beth firmly. 'I have brought some with me and we shall drink it from proper glasses. It is a small ritual I always insist on when we hand over a completed order…a superstition we have that it is bad luck not to do so.'

'Er… I…' Beth had some pretty champagne flutes made of the same glass and in the same style as her new window display. Quickly she went to get them, reflecting ruefully that it would be far more appropriate to be using Waterford crystal—only her personal finances did not run to such luxuries.

Although Alex's aunt did raise her eyebrows a little at the glasses Beth produced, to Beth's relief she did not raise any objections.

This whole situation was completely surreal, Beth decided dizzily as Alex's aunt uncorked the champagne with a deftness that left Beth in awe. The van driver and the chauffeur had been dismissed, and only the two of them were left in the shop.

'You will open this first box,' Beth was instructed as Alex's aunt removed the top package from the nearest packing case.

Obediently Beth did as she was told, her fingers trembling slightly as she eased the carefully wrapped glass out of a box of six.

The theatricality with which Alex's aunt was surrounding the whole event was impossibly dramatic. Beth could just imagine the chaos it would cause if she were to react to every delivery they received like this. But once the glass was free of its covering, and she could see it properly, any irritation she had felt at Alex's aunt's high-handedness was banished.

A soft breath of pure, awed appreciation slid from Beth's parted lips as she drank in the beauty of the glass she was cradling. The shop's lighting made every cut facet sparkle and shimmer with the rich cranberry colour of the goblet-shaped bowl, its stem clear and pure and worked with the most intricate design of trailing ivy and grapes.

Here was a reproduction Venetian glass of truly outstanding authenticity, a fruitful marriage of ancient and modern. Wonderingly Beth ran her fingertips over it. It was, quite simply, one of the most beautiful glasses she had ever seen, if anything even better and richer than the original antique she had been shown by the gypsy.

'It is good…yes?' Alex's aunt was saying, her voice softer and more gentle as she recognised what Beth was feeling.

Beth looked up at her and saw in her eyes the same love that she herself always felt for a thing of such outstanding beauty.

'It is very good,' she agreed simply, blinking back the emotional tears that had filled her eyes.

'Ah, yes, now I see why Alex has chosen you,' she heard his aunt telling her. 'Now I see that you are one of us. This is my own design, adapted from an original, of course. I think that the vine and the grapes are a truly authentic touch for a glass designed for wine. My cousins feel it is perhaps a little too modern, but I have brought for you also some much more traditional baroque designs. You will love them all.'

'I *will* love them all,' Beth confirmed shakily, 'but I cannot possibly keep them. I can't afford…'

'I have to go. I am to have dinner with Alex's parents this evening…'

'Please,' Beth begged her. 'I cannot accept this order. I must ask you to take it away.' As she saw the look of incomprehension darken Alex's aunt's eyes, Beth spread her hands helplessly and told her shakily, 'I would love to keep it, but I simply cannot afford to pay for such an order…'

'Did I not explain?' the older woman asked her, frowning. 'There is to be no question of payment.' She added firmly, 'This is a gift.'

'A gift!' Beth stared at her, the colour leaving her face, her chin lifting as pride stiffened her body. 'That is very generous of you but I simply could not accept. For you to give me such a gift is…'

'Oh, but it is not from me. I am a businesswoman,' she told Beth sturdily. 'Not even to my own family would I make such a gesture. My finest glass—*and* my order books and workforce totally disrupted to do it. No…it is *Alex* who makes the gift to you. I told him that he must love you very much indeed. I know he is not poor—his grandfather was a wealthy man, who prospered here in his adoptive country— but Alex is an academic who will never earn himself a fortune. But who can set a price on love? Although at first I was inclined to tell him that what he asked for was impossible, when he explained to me that without this order you would lose your business, which you love so very much, I could see that your pain would be his and I gave in to the sentimental side of my nature. I am sorry, but I really must go. And remember, you are not to open my gift to you until you are together with Alex. You and he will know the right time…'

The glass was a gift from Alex. *Alex* had paid for all of this… As Alex's aunt left the shop and headed for her Mercedes Beth stared around herself.

It was impossible for her to accept, of course. Even more so now that she knew Alex had paid for everything out of his own pocket.

Her heart started to race and thud erratically as she dwelt on the implications of what he had done.

His aunt had seemed to assume that their feelings for one another were an acknowledged and estab- lished thing. Had Alex told her that? 'He loves you,' she had told Beth. 'It is very much a tradition that the men of our family fall in love at first sight.'

What if she was right? What if Alex *had*, as he had claimed, fallen in love with her…? She had been wrong about his motivation in trying to dissuade her from buying via the gypsies; she knew that now. What if she had been wrong in other ways as well? What if…?

The doorbell rang, alerting her to the fact that she was no longer alone. As she turned round she started to smile in welcome relief as she saw that her visitor was her godmother, Anna.

'My goodness, this looks very exciting!' Anna exclaimed curiously as she closed the shop door behind her. 'Ward and I were just on our way back from Yorkshire and I saw that the shop lights were on so I got him to drop me off.'

Anna and her husband Ward were looking for a new house in the area, and in the meantime they were spending their time between Ward's house in Yorkshire and Anna's existing home in Rye-on-Averton.

'Come and sit down,' Beth advised her godmother affectionately as she saw the way Anna was rubbing her side. She and Ward were expecting their first baby and Beth looked a little enviously at her, noting how well pregnancy suited her. Of course, it helped having a husband who idolised and adored you, and who thought you were the cleverest person in the whole world simply because you were carrying his child.

'That's what happens when you get to be first-time parents at our age,' Anna laughed whenever people remarked on how thrilled Ward was about their coming baby.

'Of course I'm pleased,' Ward had announced promptly once in Beth's hearing when someone had raised the subject. 'But no matter how much I shall love our daughter or our son, once he or she arrives, I couldn't possibly love them anywhere near as much as I do Anna…'

For a normally slightly dour man it had been an extremely open and emotional thing to say, and at the time she had heard it Beth hadn't been able to help reflecting on how wonderful it must be to know that one was so deeply and sincerely loved. She had gone home that night and had wept a little in the lonely secrecy of her bed, still denying to herself that Alex had meant anything to her.

'Your order has arrived, then,' Anna commented, and then caught her breath on a sharp exclamation of pleasure as she saw the glass that Beth had already unpacked.

'Oh, Beth, it's beautiful,' she half whispered in awe. 'I must confess when you told us about it I couldn't imagine…I *didn't* imagine just how wonderful it would actually be. This is exquisite…'

'Exquisite, expensive and not actually my order,' Beth told her ruefully.

'Oh?'

'It's a long story,' Beth protested, shaking her head a little in denial of the questioning look she could see in her godmother's eyes.

'I've got time—plenty of time,' Anna assured her.

It would be a relief to tell someone exactly what had happened, Beth admitted, especially if that someone was her loving, gently non-judgemental godmother.

'Well, it's like this…' she began.

*   *   *

'And so you see,' Beth concluded, when she had finished explaining to Anna just what had happened, 'there's no way I can keep the glass, nor accept such an expensive present...'

'Not even from the man you love?' Anna suggested gently.

Beth flushed, shaking her head.

'*Especially* not from the man I love,' she objected. 'I just don't know what I'm going to do, Anna, how I'm going to explain...'

'Well, I can't give you any advice other than to tell you to follow your heart, to listen *with* your heart and your emotions.'

'But I can't just tell him that I love him. I can't say that I lied...that I want him...that I...'

'Why not?' Anna asked her mildly. 'You've told *me*!'

CHAPTER TEN

WHY not indeed?

Beth gnawed on her bottom lip. Anna had gone and she was on her own; the shop was locked and she had made herself a meal which she had been totally unable to eat. It was now just gone seven o'clock. She had Alex's address and his telephone number because they were written on the delivery note that came with the glass. All she had to do was pick up the phone and dial.

And then what? Tell him, I love you, Alex. I was wrong about you, about everything, and now I can tell you that I've loved you all the time. Now I can allow myself to admit that I love you? Would he believe her? And even if he did how would he feel about the paucity of her gesture, her *love*, when compared with the rich generosity of his? It wasn't that she loved him any less than he did her; that was impossible. Her love was just as deep, just as committed…just as intense. It was just that her previous experience had made her wary of giving too much too soon, and meeting him had in one sense come too soon on top of her realisation of Julian's perfidy.

At least Alex would never be able to accuse her of using him as…

She started to dial his number and then stopped. Perhaps tomorrow, after she had had time to think properly, to rehearse what she needed to say…or maybe… She had taken the gift-wrapped box his aunt had given her upstairs, and her attention was caught by it. She went over to it and picked it up. It was heavy. 'You will open it with Alex…when you are together,' she had told Beth.

Suddenly a very daring and dangerous plan occurred to her. Without giving herself time to change her mind, Beth picked up the box and grabbed her coat and her car keys.

Lexminster wasn't that far away—a two-hour drive, maybe even less at this time of night.

Alex picked up some papers he had brought home to work on. His mother had telephoned earlier, inviting him over for dinner.

'Your aunt will be here, but only for the one night; she's flying on to New York tomorrow…'

Alex had been tempted, but he had already endured one very stern lecture from her on his foolhardiness and stubborn persistence in persuading her to give priority to his order for Beth. When would she receive it? he wondered. His aunt had promised, albeit reluctantly, that she would have it in time for the Christmas market.

He wasn't quite sure how Beth would react when she *did* receive it. It wasn't entirely impossible that she would send it back to him in a million broken pieces, but he suspected that it might be that she couldn't bring herself to destroy something which he knew already she would find irresistibly beautiful.

He had made himself a meal earlier but had not really felt like eating it. God, but he ached for Beth. Somehow, and he didn't know quite how yet, he was going to find a way to convince her that he loved her, that he was genuine and that she loved him—because Alex was convinced that she did. She might claim that all they had shared had been sex, but Alex knew her, and she simply wasn't that kind of woman. Her emotions ran too deep and too strong for her to divorce herself from them like that. She could not have responded to him the way she had without feeling something for him. He was convinced of it.

He frowned as he heard his doorbell ring. He wasn't really in the mood for company. He got up and walked from his living room into the hallway and opened the front door.

'Beth!'

Beth stood nervously in the doorway, her nervousness increased by the shock she could see in Alex's eyes and hear in his voice.

'I...' She took a step backwards and looked wildly over her shoulder, as though about to flee.

Immediately Alex reached for her wrist, drawing her gently but firmly inside and closing the door behind her.

Beneath his grasp her wrist-bones felt heart-wrenchingly fragile. Under her free arm she was clutching a large rectangular parcel against her body.

'A present...for me...?' he asked teasingly, trying to lighten her tension.

'No, actually it's for me...from your aunt,' Beth told him in a disjointed, almost staccato little burst of speech. 'She said you would have one too and that we had to open them together. Alex, why did you do...why did you send me the glass? You must know that I can't accept it...'

To her own consternation her eyes filled with tears. Whilst she was talking Alex had been urging her along his hallway and was now ushering her into a beautifully proportioned room which, in some obscure way, reminded her of the drawing room in the castle. Her face started to burn, her heart thumping at the memories she was evoking.

'Come and sit down and we'll talk about it,' Alex suggested, relieving her of her coat and guiding her towards a softly upholstered and very deep sofa.

A little unsteadily Beth sank into it. In addition to relieving her of her coat Alex had also relieved her of the cumbersome parcel.

When he returned he was carrying two glasses.

'It's brandy,' he told her. 'Drink it; it will help you to relax a bit…'

Dutifully Beth took a sip and then pulled a face.

'I've already had champagne with your aunt,' she told him as she put her glass down. 'Perhaps the two don't mix. Alex…I can't accept your gift. It's wonderful…the glass is beautiful, even more beautiful than I could have imagined, but why…why did you do it?' she asked him, abandoning the reasoned, rational argument she had prepared and doing instead what Anna had urged her to do and responding only to her emotions.

'Didn't my aunt tell you?' Alex asked her ruefully. He hadn't thought that his aunt would hand Beth's glass over to her in person, but then realistically he should perhaps have guessed that it was the kind of thing she would do. She was extremely picky about whom she allowed to have her precious glass, and, of course, Alex's own admissions to her had aroused her curiosity about Beth to an even greater intensity.

Beth hesitated, unable to look at him.

'She said…she said it was because you loved me,' she told him huskily. She could feel Alex looking at her, and her own gaze was drawn to his, her face flushing as she saw the look in his eyes.

'And did you believe her?' he asked her quietly.

Beth bit her lip.

'I…' She felt as though she was drowning, losing control, fighting to prevent herself from being swept under by the force of her own emotions, afraid of their power—and yet at the same time a part of her was longing to give in, to give up, to let someone else carry the burden of her loving for her.

'I…I wanted to,' she admitted truthfully.

'Why…because you wanted to have more sex with me?' Alex couldn't resist probing, a little unkindly.

Beth reacted as though he had actually physically hurt her, her breath leaking from her lungs, her face draining of colour, even her hand going out as though to ward off an actual blow.

'Oh, Beth…my love, my precious, precious love, I'm sorry,' Alex apologised remorsefully. 'I didn't mean—'

'No. No…it's all right. I know I deserved it,' Beth interrupted him jerkily. 'I shouldn't have come here.' She tried to get up, desperate to escape before she completed her own humiliation by bursting into tears. She had got it all wrong. Alex didn't love her at all. His aunt had got it all wrong.

'What you deserve is to be cherished and loved,

adored, worshipped,' Alex was telling her extravagantly.

'Alex,' she protested.

'How could you *possibly* think I didn't mean it?'
Alex overrode her protest tenderly. 'Have you any
idea how much I've missed you, how many times
I've been tempted to come and find you, capture you,
kidnap you, bear you off with me to my lair as one
of my ancestors might have done?'

'I can't imagine you ever displaying such cave-
man-like tactics,' Beth told him ruefully. 'You…'

'No? Watch me,' Alex mock-threatened her, and
then, before she could speak, he was reaching for her,
wrapping her in his arms, kissing her with a passion
that broke through all her resistance.

She tried to speak, to protest…plead for time and
explanations, but her words were lost, silenced beneath the hungry pressure of his mouth that only re-
laxed when she made a tiny sound. Whilst he was
kissing her he dropped his arms to his sides, sliding
his fingers between hers so that they were standing
body to body, arm to arm, only their heads, their lips
moving. Her own body was trembling with increas-
ing intensity as she reacted to his closeness. Her body
was betraying her far more than any words, Beth
knew.

'"Just sex" could never feel like this,' Alex whispered thickly against her mouth. '"Just sex" could
never make me want you the way I do, and it could
never make you respond to me the way you are.'

'Alex, I got it all wrong,' Beth told him guiltily.
'I totally misjudged you and I misjudged my own
feelings as well, totally and wilfully. I thought—'

'I know what you *thought*,' Alex interrupted her. 'But what is more interesting right now is what you *felt*...what you are feeling... Or shall I discover for myself?'

She was wearing a soft buttoned cardigan, and as Alex started to trace the vee of flesh it exposed Beth's whole body began to quiver. Her desire for him drenched her, flooded her, melted her; she was reaching eagerly for him long before he had finished unbuttoning her cardigan, and touching him long, long before his hands had started to cup her naked breasts, stroking them, his fingers plucking delicately at her tight nipples.

'Tell me you love me,' he demanded thickly against her breast as he slid to his knees in front of her.

'I love you... I love you... I... Oh, Alex, Alex,' Beth gasped, torn between shock and fierce arousal as he pulled off her skirt and slid his hands up under her briefs to cup the rounded shape of her buttocks whilst his tongue-tip rimmed her navel. She knew what would happen next, what she *wanted* to happen next. Just thinking about how it had felt to have his breath, his mouth, his tongue against that part of her body made her shudder from head to foot in explosive yearning.

They made love quickly and fiercely, like two starving people attacking a banquet, their appetites too hungry to be easily sated and yet their stomachs too shrunken by deprivation for the endurance required to eat their leisurely fill.

All they could manage was a taste here, a mouthful there, a gulp of love's rich, raw wine before they were both crying out in their need for completion. It came swiftly, hotly, rawly almost, Beth acknowledged as she lay panting and light-headed in Alex's arms.

Later, when he carried her to bed, she protested, 'I can't…I've got to go home. It's late—the shop…'

'You can. I am now your home. The shop can wait…we can't…'

This time they did their personal sensual banquet full justice, eating appreciatively of every course, true connoisseurs of what was set before them.

'What do you suppose is in the parcel?' Beth asked Alex drowsily just before she finally fell asleep in his arms.

'We shall have to wait and see. Remember we can't open them until I have mine.'

'Mmm… Alex, have I told you how much I love you?'

'Many times,' Alex assured her gently, knowing just why she asked.

'I never really loved Julian Cox, you know,' Beth assured him. 'It was just… I wanted to be in love with him…I wanted to believe him…'

'Forget him. He doesn't matter to us,' Alex told her.

Beth gave a soft sigh of contented pleasure. She loved it that Alex felt so secure with her, that he could accept her honest admission that she had made a mistake.

'I always knew you were plotting to make me have your aunt's glass,' she teased him lovingly as she reached out to trace the shape of his mouth with her fingertip.

As he nipped and nibbled at her probing finger Alex replied. 'No, you're wrong,' he denied, and then he said softly, 'What I've been plotting ever since I first saw you is to get you so that I can do this…'

As he rolled her over on top of him Beth protested, torn between excitement and laughter.

'Alex, we can't…not again…'

'Oh, yes, we can,' he assured her. 'Oh, yes, we can!'

EPILOGUE

'WELL, shall we open them, then?' Alex asked Beth provocatively.

It was Christmas Eve and they were in Alex's apartment. They were due to spend Christmas Day with Alex's parents and Boxing Day with her own. Tonight, though, they were spending on their own. On her ring finger was the flawlessly cut diamond Alex had just given her. They had chosen it together the previous week and now, as she reached out her hands towards him to take the mysterious parcel his aunt had left with her, it caught the light, flooding the space around them with prisms of colour.

They were going to get married in the spring, here in England, and then they were going to fly to Prague for a very special family celebration which would be held at the castle.

'Another family tradition?' Beth had teased Alex when he had first mentioned it to her.

'Not exactly, but I know it would mean a lot to the family…'

'And to me,' Beth had told him seriously, her eyes full of love.

Now, as they both unwrapped their parcels, she couldn't help reflecting how very, very lucky she was. It chilled her blood to think how easily she might not have met Alex at all.

Inside the wrapping paper was a cardboard box. Quickly she unfastened it and reached inside, and then waited. Alex was watching her, his own box still unopened.

'We have to open them together,' she reminded him sternly, and then, as she saw his face, she accused him, 'You know what it is, don't you?'

'It's a family tradition,' Alex replied, his expression mock-injured.

'Oh, you,' Beth protested, reaching inside her box, the laughter in her eyes stilled as she removed its contents.

It was a lustre, just like the one she had first seen in the hotel gift shop but even more beautiful.

'Oh, Alex,' she whispered as she studied it. 'Oh, Alex, it's beautiful…'

'*They* are beautiful,' Alex corrected her, removing his own from its packaging and putting it next to hers. 'A perfect pair…like us,' he added as he bent his head to kiss her.

'A perfect pair…' Beth sighed in blissful happiness. 'Oh, Alex,' she whispered.

'Oh, Beth,' Alex whispered back, and then added engagingly, 'Do you think we might just check that it isn't just sex…one more time…?'

'It's only eight o'clock. Far too early for bed yet,' Beth protested, but her eyes were shining and there was no reluctance whatsoever in her expression as she clung lovingly to him…quite the opposite.

A perfect pair. Oh, yes, indeed… Oh, yes… Yes… Yes…

'Mmm…'

Look for Dee's story,
THE MARRIAGE RESOLUTION,
coming soon from Mills & Boon

MILLS & BOON®

Makes any time special

Enjoy a romantic novel from
Mills & Boon®

Presents...™   *Enchanted*™   *Temptation*®

Historical Romance™   *Medical Romance*™

MILLS & BOON®

Next Month's Romance Titles

♡

Each month you can choose from a wide variety of romance novels from Mills & Boon®. Below are the new titles to look out for next month from the Presents...™ and Enchanted™ series.

Presents...™

A BOSS IN A MILLION	Helen Brooks
HAVING LEO'S CHILD	Emma Darcy
THE BABY DEAL	Alison Kelly
THE SEDUCTION BUSINESS	Charlotte Lamb
THE WEDDING-NIGHT AFFAIR	Miranda Lee
REFORM OF THE PLAYBOY	Mary Lyons
MORE THAN A MISTRESS	Sandra Marton
THE MARRIAGE EXPERIMENT	Catherine Spencer

Enchanted™

TYCOON FOR HIRE	Lucy Gordon
MARRYING MR RIGHT	Carolyn Greene
THE WEDDING COUNTDOWN	Barbara Hannay
THE BOSS AND THE PLAIN JAYNE BRIDE	Heather MacAllister
THE RELUCTANT GROOM	Emma Richmond
READY, SET...BABY	Christie Ridgway
THE ONE-WEEK MARRIAGE	Renee Roszel
UNDERCOVER BABY	Rebecca Winters

On sale from 3rd September 1999

H1 9908

Available at most branches of WH Smith, Tesco, Asda, Martins, Borders, Easons, Volume One/James Thin and most good paperback bookshops

MILLS & BOON®

MEDICAL ROMANCE™

HER PASSION FOR DR JONES by Lilian Darcy
Southshore - No.1 of 4

Dr Harry Jones is sure it's a mistake having Rebecca Irwin work in the practice. Despite the raging attraction between her and Harry, Rebecca fought her corner!

BACHELOR CURE by Marion Lennox
Bachelor Doctors

Dr Tessa Westcott burst into Mike Llewellyn's life like a red-headed whirlwind. She said exactly what she thought, and turned his ordered world upside down. It couldn't last. But Mike had to admit, she lightened his life.

HOLDING THE BABY by Laura MacDonald

Lewis's sister was abroad and he was left holding the baby—literally! He *badly* needed help with the three children and asked Jo Henry to be nanny. In a family situation, Jo and Lewis became *vividly* aware of each other...

SEVENTH DAUGHTER by Gill Sanderson

Specialist registrar Dr James Owen was everything Dr Delyth Price ever wanted in a man. But Delyth had a gift not everyone understood. James seemed prepared to listen, if not to believe. Then she discovered his lighthearted side, and fell even deeper into love...

Available from 3rd September 1999

Available at most branches of WH Smith, Tesco, Asda, Martins, Borders, Easons, Volume One/James Thin and most good paperback bookshops

Spoil yourself next month
with these four novels from

TEMPTATION

MACKENZIE'S WOMAN by JoAnn Ross

Bachelor Auction

Kate Campbell had to persuade Alec Mackenzie to take part in a
charity bachelor auction. This rugged adventurer would have
women bidding millions for an hour of his time. Trouble was,
Alec wasn't really a bachelor. Though nobody knew it—he was
married to Kate!

A PRIVATE EYEFUL by Ruth Jean Dale

Hero for Hire

Nick Charles was a bodyguard on a vital assignment. But no one
had yet told him exactly what that assignment was! So he was
hanging around a luxury resort, waiting… Then along came
luscious Cory Leblanc and Nick just knew she was a prime
candidate—for *something*…

PRIVATE LESSONS by Julie Elizabeth Leto

Blaze

'Harley' turned up on Grant Riordan's doorstep and sent his
libido skyrocketing. Hired as the 'entertainment' for a bachelor
party, she was dressed like an exotic dancer but had the eyes of
an innocent. Unfortunately, after a little accident, she didn't
have a clue who she was…

SEDUCING SYDNEY by Kathy Marks

Plain-Jane Sydney Stone was feeling seriously out of place in a
glamorous Las Vegas hotel, when she received a mysterious
note arranging a date—for that night! She was sure the message
must have been delivered to the wrong woman. But maybe
she'd just go and find out…

Our hottest

TEMPTATION

authors bring you…

Blaze

**Three sizzling love stories available in
one volume in September 1999.**

Midnight Heat
JoAnn Ross

A Lark in the Dark
Heather MacAllister

Night Fire
Elda Minger

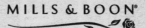

4 Books
and a surprise gift!

We would like to take this opportunity to thank you for reading this Mills & Boon® book by offering you the chance to take FOUR more specially selected titles from the Presents...™ series absolutely FREE! We're also making this offer to introduce you to the benefits of the Reader Service™—

> ★ FREE home delivery
> ★ FREE gifts and competitions
> ★ FREE monthly Newsletter
> ★ Books available before they're in the shops
> ★ Exclusive Reader Service discounts

Accepting these FREE books and gift places you under no obligation to buy; you may cancel at any time, even after receiving your free shipment. Simply complete your details below and return the entire page to the address below. *You don't even need a stamp!*

YES! Please send me 4 free Presents...™ books and a surprise gift. I understand that unless you hear from me, I will receive 6 superb new titles every month for just £2.40 each, postage and packing free. I am under no obligation to purchase any books and may cancel my subscription at any time. The free books and gift will be mine to keep in any case.

P9EB

Ms/Mrs/Miss/Mr ....Initials...
BLOCK CAPITALS PLEASE

Surname...

Address...

....

....Postcode ....

Send this whole page to:
THE READER SERVICE, FREEPOST CN81, CROYDON, CR9 3WZ
(Eire readers please send coupon to: P.O. Box 4546, KILCOCK, COUNTY KILDARE)

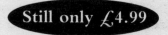